Lawman on the Hunt

CINDI MYERS

First Published in Great Britain 2016
By Mills & Boon, an imprint of HarperCollins*Publishers*
1 London Bridge Street, London, SE1 9GF

Large Print edition 2016

© 2016 Cynthia Myers

ISBN: 978-0-263-06661-6

Our policy is to use papers that are natural, renewable
and recyclable products and made from wood grown
in sustainable forests. The logging and manufacturing
processes conform to the legal environmental
regulations of the country of origin.

Printed and bound in Great Britain
by CPI Antony Rowe, Chippenham, Wiltshire

"You okay?"

"Yeah." He raised his head, then sat up. The ledge they had come to rest on was safe enough for some of the tension to ease out of him.

She struggled into a sitting position and glared at him. "What did you think you were doing, tackling me that way? You could have been killed."

"I had to save you."

She wiped away a smear of blood and mud on her cheek. "No, you didn't. You'd be better off without me. You could move faster on your own."

"No, I wouldn't be better off without you." He shifted to kneel in front of her and grabbed both her arms. "I never was."

He told himself he deserved the wary look she gave him. He had certainly given her plenty of reasons to not believe him, to be afraid of him, even. He smoothed his hands down her arms, then gently pulled her to him. "I need you, Leah," he whispered. "I always have."

Cindi Myers is the author of more than fifty novels. When she's not crafting new romance plots, she enjoys skiing, gardening, cooking, crafting and daydreaming. A lover of small-town life, she lives with her husband and two spoiled dogs in the Colorado mountains.

Chapter One

Special Agent Travis Steadman studied the house through military-grade field glasses. Situated on a wooded escarpment above a rushing stream, the sprawling log home afforded its occupants a sweeping view of the snow-dusted Colorado mountains and the golden valley below. Sun glaring on the expanse of glass in the front of the house prevented Travis from seeing inside, but the intel reports told him all he needed to know. The two men and one woman who had rented the house two weeks ago looked like wealthy second-home owners enjoying a quiet mountain retreat, but the FBI suspected they were part of a dangerous terrorist cell.

"One car leaving. Looks like Braeswood and Roland." The crisp words, from fellow agent Luke Renfro, sounded clear in Travis's earpiece.

"I see them," he replied as a black Cadillac Escalade nosed out of the steep driveway. Through the side windows he could make out Duane Braeswood's sharp-nosed profile and Eddie Roland's bullet-shaped shaved head. "They're turning left, toward the highway to Durango."

"Here comes the woman and her driver," Luke said. "I wonder why she didn't go with them."

"Maybe she's going shopping. Or to get her hair done." Travis tried to keep any sign of tension out of his voice, even as he raised the glasses again to focus on the Toyota sedan that halted briefly at the bottom of the drive. He could just make out the silhouettes of the male driver and the woman beside him, but he didn't need the glasses to fill in the details about her. Leah Carlisle was twenty-seven years old, with thick dark hair that curled when she didn't straighten it, which she usually did. Her brown eyes, the color of good coffee with cream, were wide-spaced and slightly almond-shaped, and she could convey a score of different emotions with merely a look. She had a good figure, with a narrow waist and a firm butt, and small but round and firm breasts that were wonderfully sensitive. She enjoyed sex, and the two of them had been really good together...

He lowered the glasses and pushed the thoughts away. Leah's car also turned left, toward town. Maybe she was going to meet up with her partners in crime in Durango. He ground his teeth together, fighting the old anger. To think she had left him to be with scum like Braeswood and Roland.

"Did you say something?" Luke asked. "Transmission's a little fuzzy on my end."

Travis feared he had growled or made some other sound to signal his frustration. He needed to get a better grip. Only Luke, his closest friend, knew about his former relationship with Leah, and he had kept this information to himself.

Travis had admitted to their boss, Special Agent in Charge Ted Blessing, that he was acquainted with Leah. After all, they were from the same hometown, and it wouldn't take a genius to figure out they had gone to school together. But no one knew he had planned to marry her. "Looks like she's headed to Durango, too," he said.

"Give them ten minutes, then we move in." Blessing's voice, deep and sonorous as a preacher's, shifted Travis's focus to the mission. He and Luke and Blessing and the other members of Search Team Seven were moving in for a "sneak and peek" at the interior of the cabin. They had wrangled a warrant that gave them onetime permission to go inside, look around and plant a couple of bugs that would, they hoped, provide the evidence they needed to arrest and convict Braeswood, Roland and Leah of terrorist activities.

The Bureau suspected the trio had ties to a series of bombings that had exploded at two major professional bicycle races around the world. Blessing and his team had stopped a third bombing attempt in Denver last month, but the bomber had died before he could give them any more information about his connections to these three.

Travis stowed the binoculars and prepared to move down from his lookout position in the rocks across from and above the house. When the signal came, Luke and Blessing would move inside with the rest of the team and Travis would station himself at the end of the driveway, alert for the premature return of the house's occupants.

"Recon Three, you hear me?" The flat, Midwestern accent of Special Agent Gus Mathers came across with the question.

"You're loud and clear," Travis answered.

"Best-case scenario, we've got an hour," Mathers said. "I don't like the looks of that drive—too steep and narrow, and situated in the curve of the road like it is, we won't have much warning if someone comes. You'll have to stall them at the bottom of the drive. Tell them we've got an explosive fuse or something."

"An explosive fuse?" He made a face. "What's that?"

"I don't know, but it sounds good, doesn't it? Something you wouldn't want to interfere with. There's nothing in these folks' backgrounds that shows they know anything about electricity. Just do what you can to keep them back if something comes up."

"Nothing will come up," Travis said. "Even if they drove to Durango and immediately turned around and came back, it would take them an hour."

"Better to be prepared. And let us know if you see anybody else suspicious."

"I know my job." And like everyone else on the team, with the exception of their commander, Blessing, he knew all the players in this case—even ones who were on the periphery or merely suspected of having some tie. The Search Team Seven members were all "super recognizers"—agents who literally never forgot a face. Travis hadn't even realized other people shared his peculiar talent until he had been recruited by the Bureau. He could see someone once, in person or on video or in a still photo, and pick them out of a crowd months later. The Bureau hoped the team would prove useful in identifying suspected criminals before they acted. So far, they had had a few successes, but this terrorist operation was their biggest operation yet.

"Okay, we're going in now." Special Agent in Charge Blessing gave the order.

Travis waited while a utility van with the logo of the local electric company moved slowly down the road and turned into the driveway of the log home. As soon as they reached the house, Luke, Blessing, Mathers and the three other team members inside would pile out and go to work. Mathers and Special Agent Jack Prescott, who had trained with the Bureau's TacOps team before transferring to Search Team Seven, would replace the living room and bedroom thermostats with identical units that contained listening devices, while Luke and Special Agent Cameron Hsung swept the premises for any incriminating evidence. Luke would download the hard drives from any computers onto a portable unit, and Hsung would photograph anything else that looked suspicious.

When Travis was confident the rest of the team was in place, he slipped across the road to the front of the house. Dressed in khaki cargo pants and a long-sleeved khaki shirt with the logo of the electric utility over the breast pocket, he would appear to anyone watching to be a utility worker repairing a malfunction or inspecting equipment. He knelt in front of the electrical box at the end of the drive and pried off the cover. He pretended to study its contents, though he was really scanning the approaches to the house. One hundred yards ahead on the same side of the road, a paved drive led to a glass-and-cedar chalet, the log home's closest neighbor. A retired couple lived there. The intel reports noted that they didn't go out much.

A soft breeze rustled in the aspens that lined

the road, sending a shower of golden leaves over him. Another month and they'd have snow here in the high country. Already the highest peaks of the San Juans showed a light dusting. Leah would be happy about that. She had grown up in Durango and liked to ski. Was that why the trio had ended up here, after abandoning the house they had rented in Denver, only a few days before their friend Danny had tried to set off a bomb at the Colorado Cycling Challenge bike race?

"Hello! Is there a problem with the electricity?"

Wrench raised like a weapon, Travis whirled to see a slender man with a head of hair like Albert Einstein step from the shrubbery beside the road and stride toward him.

"Our sensors indicated some bad wiring." He lowered the wrench and delivered the line smoothly, though he had no idea where the words had come from. What sensors? Did electrical wiring have sensors? "We've got a crew up at the house checking it out."

The man glanced up the driveway, a worried vee between his bushy eyebrows. "I saw the van from my house. Did Mr. and Mrs. Ellison give you permission to enter their home while they're away?" he asked.

Ellison was the alias Braeswood had adopted in Denver and was sticking with here in Durango. The "Mr. and Mrs." made Travis wince inwardly. Leah hadn't married the guy, had she? Six months had scarcely passed since she returned Travis's ring.

He realized the old man was waiting for an answer. "It's less disruptive for us to do the work while they're out of the house," Travis said. Undercover Tactics 101: know how to bluff.

The man's frown morphed into a glare. "I

didn't ask whether or not it was convenient for you. Did you get their permission?"

"I'm sure my supervisor spoke to them," he said. He made a show of focusing once more on the interior of the utility box, though every nerve was attuned to the old man and his reaction. All he needed was for this guy to decide to phone the utility company and ask about the group of "workers." Or worse, this nosy neighbor might decide to call Leah or her "husband." Even thinking the word made his stomach churn.

"Does this have anything to do with the power outages we had last week?" the man asked. "I called twice to report them, and the woman on the phone said they would check things out, but you all are the first workers I've seen."

"I'm sorry, I don't know the answer to that." Travis tried to look friendly and humble. "I'm new on the job."

"I thought as much," the man said. "You're going to electrocute yourself if you tear into that box with an uninsulated wrench like that."

Cursing his own ignorance—and the TacOps unit for not doing a better job of briefing him— he dropped the wrench and took out a pair of pliers, the handles bound in green insulating rubber.

"I'm not sure Lisa would be happy to have you all in her house while she's out," the man continued.

So he knew her as Lisa. Close enough to her real name to avoid confusion. Or maybe the old man had misremembered. *No, I'm sure she wouldn't like having us in her house,* Travis thought. He glanced down the road, which was empty, then sat back on his heels and looked up at the man. "I thought I heard they just moved in," he said.

"That's right. They've only been here a couple of weeks. But I made a point of going over to meet them. I think it's always a good idea to know your neighbors."

So he didn't go out much, but he definitely kept tabs on everything. That might make him a useful witness in court one day. "Uh-huh." What could he say to get rid of this guy?

"Her husband was a little standoffish, but she was sweet as could be. As beautiful inside as she is outside."

Yeah, she fooled me into thinking that once, too. He turned back toward the electrical box. "It's been great talking to you," he said. "But I'd better get back to work. We should be out of your way pretty quickly."

"All right." The man leaned closer to peer at him. "Duke G. What does the G stand for?"

"Graham." Travis glanced at the name embroidered into the shirt. He had no idea who Duke

Graham was. It was merely the name someone in the props department for TacOps had chosen.

The old man moved back up the road and turned into his driveway. Travis stood and walked up the driveway a short way, until he was sure the neighbor was out of sight. Then he pulled out his phone.

"What is it?" Gus answered halfway through the first ring.

"The next-door neighbor was over here nosing around. I'd hurry it up if I were you."

"We'll wrap it up as soon as we can, but we don't want to abort if we don't have to. We aren't likely to get another warrant."

"Just thought I'd give you a heads-up."

"Thanks." He disconnected, and Travis pocketed his phone and returned to the end of the driveway.

Five minutes later, his knees were beginning to ache from crouching in front of the utility box when a white Toyota sedan came roaring around the curve and swept into the driveway. Travis didn't have time to leap out of sight into the bushes or pull out his phone or weapon before the car screeched to a halt and the passenger window rolled down. Leah stared at him, but said nothing. She appeared stunned.

Her hair was longer than he remembered, and she was maybe a little thinner, but she was still as beautiful as ever. He hated the way his heart ached when her eyes met his. She had dumped him with no explanation and had never looked back. He had thought that betrayal had burned away all the love he had felt for her, but apparently there was enough feeling left that he could still hurt.

He stood and moved toward her. He had one job now, and that was to keep her away from the house until the team finished their work.

"Hello, ma'am," he said, his voice flat, betraying nothing.

She gripped the edge of the window with both hands, her knuckles white. She wore red polish on her nails to match the scarlet of her sweater, but some of the polish was chipped. Unlike her. She was usually perfectly put together. "Who are you?" The driver—a burly man who wore a knit cap pulled low over his forehead—leaned across Leah to glare at Travis.

"There's a problem with the power," Travis said, still watching Leah out of the corner of his eye. "We should have it repaired shortly."

"I don't believe you."

Time seemed to speed up after that. The driver reached under his jacket. "Down, Leah!" Travis yelled as he drew his own weapon. She shoved open the passenger door and dropped to the ground as he and the driver exchanged fire. Travis dived for the cover of the electrical box as

Leah rolled toward the ditch. The driver revved the car and veered off the driveway, crashing into the underbrush.

In the silence that followed, Travis studied the slumped figure of the driver and decided he had been wounded, or maybe killed. He needed to check on the man in a minute, but first he had to deal with Leah. She crawled to him. "Travis, what are you doing here?" she asked.

"Maybe I wanted to see you," he said. "Maybe I wanted to ask why you couldn't even bring yourself to say goodbye to my face."

Two bright spots of color bloomed on her pale cheeks, as if she were feverish. "I thought it would be easier if I left quietly."

"You left me a letter. A freaking Dear John letter, like some bad movie cliché." The diamond engagement ring he had given her only six weeks before had sat beside the letter, another bullet to his heart.

"I really don't think we should be talking about this." She glanced up the drive toward the wrecked car. "I have to go."

He moved in front of her. "I think it's past time we talked." This really wasn't the best place for this conversation, but he couldn't keep the words back. "I loved you. I thought you loved me. We were going to be married, and then one day I get home and all I've got left of you is a note on the kitchen counter." The note had read *I'm sorry, but I've changed my mind. Please don't come after me. This is for the best. Love, Leah.* The "love" had trailed off at the end, as if her hand had shaken as she'd written it.

She wouldn't look at him, staring instead at the ground. Her hair was coming undone from its ponytail, and she had a streak of dirt across her cheek. "Sometimes things aren't meant to be," she said.

"Are you married to Braeswood now? Or should I call him Ellison?"

She jerked her head toward him, her eyes wide. "No! Why would you think that?"

"The neighbor called you Mrs. Ellison."

"Oh, that. That's just…" But she didn't say what it was. He filled in the blank. Her cover story. The lies they told to hide their terrible purpose here.

"I get that you don't love me anymore," he said, letting that harsh truth fuel his anger. "But I don't understand this. Do you know what Duane Braeswood and his friend Eddie do? They're terrorists. They kill people. It's fine if you want to hate me, but do you hate your country, too?"

She bowed her head and closed her eyes. "I know what they do," she said softly. "And I don't expect you to understand."

"You're right, I don't understand." He leaned toward her, his face so close to hers he could smell her perfume. An image flashed in his mind of her naked, her body soft against his, his nose buried in the satiny skin of her throat, inhaling that floral, feminine scent.

He blinked to clear his head, and the blare of a horn yanked him back to the present. He looked past her, down the road, where the Escalade was barreling toward them. "I have to go," she said, and turned as if to run.

He snagged her arm and dragged her with him into the underbrush, seconds before the Escalade screamed into the drive.

Chapter Two

Travis had a glimpse of Duane Braeswood at the wheel, his face a mask of rage, as the SUV flew by.

He retreated farther into the underbrush. One arm wrapped around Leah, holding her to his chest, he used his free hand to pull out his phone. "Abort!" he shouted as soon as Gus answered. "Braeswood and Roland are here. And two other guys. I didn't get a look at them." They had been only dark figures in the backseat of the SUV.

Gunfire reverberated in the trees before he

had the phone back in his pocket. "Let me go!" Leah pleaded, and struggled against him.

"You're under arrest." He pulled a flex-cuff from his back pocket and wrestled it over her wrists.

"No!" she wailed, but he cut off the cry by pulling out his handkerchief and stuffing it in her mouth. She glared at him, her brown eyes almost black with rage.

"Don't worry, it's clean," he said. "The last thing I need is you letting the others know where I am."

He debated binding her ankles also and leaving her out here in the woods, but if the fight moved in this direction, she might get caught in cross fire. Besides, he didn't trust her not to find a way to escape. Better to keep her with him.

He dragged her up the steep slope toward the house. The blasts of gunfire became almost constant as they neared the building, and when they reached the edge of the clearing his heart twisted at the sight of a khaki-clad figure slumped in the drive. He couldn't tell which member of the team had been hit, but knowing they had lost one of their own was enough to make him want to get back at these guys.

He checked his weapon. The Glock wasn't going to be of much use at this range. What he wouldn't give for a sighted rifle right now. He would sit here and pick the bad guys off as they exited the house.

He looked at Leah again. Tears glistened on her cheeks, and he had to harden himself against the pain in her eyes. "Killing a federal agent is punishable by life in prison," he said. "You can be convicted of felony murder even if you didn't fire the shot, simply by your association with these killers."

Something flickered in her eyes—regret? Fear? He once thought he knew her better than anyone, that he could always read what she was thinking. But that was obviously only one of the many things he had been wrong about when it came to her.

He turned away from her to study the house again. Several windows had been shot out. At one, long drapes fluttered in the breeze. The gunfire had ceased, but he thought he heard someone moving around in there. What was the best way for him to help the agents inside? Braeswood and his men would probably expect an attack from the front, but if he could get around back he might be able to reach his trapped fellow agents.

"Is there a back door?" he asked. "Another way inside?"

She nodded.

"How do I get to it?" He pulled the handkerchief out of her mouth so she could answer, but

remained ready to stuff it back in if she started
to yell.

"There's a path through the woods, on the
side," she said softly. She nodded toward the
west side of the house. "The door leads into the
garage. There's a back door, too, but it leads
from an enclosed patio. You can't get to it without being seen from the house."

"Right. Here we go then." He started to stuff
the handkerchief back in.

"Don't," she said. "I won't say anything, I
promise."

"Since when can I trust your promises?" He
replaced the handkerchief in her mouth, ignoring the hurt that lanced him at her injured look.

He took her arm and led her around the house
toward the back door, keeping out of sight of
anyone inside. His phone vibrated and he answered it.

"Recon Three, this is Recon One. Where are

you?" Blessing spoke in a whisper, but his voice carried clearly in the silence around them.

"Outside the house. West side."

"They've got us pinned down on the second floor. Looks like a rec room. Did you say there's four of them?"

He looked to Leah for confirmation. *Four?* he mouthed. She nodded. "That's right. Braeswood, Roland, and two others," he said.

"It's too high up to jump out of the window, though it may come to that," Blessing said.

Leah tugged on his arm. He shook her off, but she tugged harder, her expression almost frantic. "Hang on a minute," he said, and pressed the phone against his chest to mute it.

He jerked the gag from her mouth. "What is it?"

"If they're in the rec room, there's a dumbwaiter," she said. "In the interior wall, behind the panel with the dartboard. It goes down to the garage."

He pressed the phone to his ear again. "Check the panel behind the dartboard," he said. "There's a dumbwaiter that goes down to the garage."

"Won't they know to block it off?" Blessing asked.

Leah shook her head. Travis muted the phone again. "They know about it, but I don't think they'll think about it," she said. "I'm the only one who uses it, when I unload groceries."

"I've got the woman with me," Travis said. "She says she's the only one who ever uses the dumbwaiter—Braeswood and the others won't remember it."

"You don't think she's setting a trap for us?" Blessing asked.

"I don't think so." Maybe that was his old

image of Leah, fooling him, but he had to trust his instincts now.

"Then we'll have to chance it." Blessing sounded older. Bone-weary. "If you can, station yourself to lay down cover fire."

"There's a side door in the garage that leads outside. I'll cover you there."

He and Leah repositioned to conceal themselves as near to the garage as he dared, taking cover first behind a propane tank, then behind a section of lattice fencing used to block trash cans from view. He half reclined, bracing his right hand on the fence. "Get down behind me," he ordered her.

"If you have another weapon, I can shoot it," she said, reminding him that he hadn't replaced her gag after his phone call with Blessing.

She knew he carried a small revolver in an ankle holster. She had certainly seen him remove it enough times when he had come home to his Adams Morgan townhome where she had spent many nights. "You may have played me for a fool before," he said. "But I'm not a big enough idiot to give a wanted felon a gun."

Anger flashed in her eyes and she opened her mouth, then apparently thought better of whatever she had been about to say and remained silent. "Get down," he ordered.

She did as he asked, reclining in the dirt behind him. The warmth of her body seeped into him, along with an awareness of the jut of her hip bone and the curve of her breast. He forced his attention back on the door. "Come on," he muttered. "Let's get this show on the road."

Long minutes passed in silence so intense he imagined he could hear the hum from the power line that connected the house with the transformer at the road. He pictured the team assembling in the garage, arriving one or two at a time via the dumbwaiter designed to carry parcels up from the garage to the living quarters. They would wait until everyone was in place before they made their exit.

"Why haven't they come out yet?" Leah whispered, when he judged twenty minutes had passed. Too long. Braeswood and company would be wondering why things in the rec room were so quiet.

"I don't know," he said.

Just then, the door from the garage eased open. Blessing's face, dark and glistening with sweat, peered out. Then the door burst all the way open and men poured out.

The first bullets thudded into the dirt around them, followed by the sickening sound of ammunition striking flesh. Heart racing, Travis scanned the area and located the source of the shots. Cursing, he fired off half a dozen quick rounds at the man stationed behind the tripod-mounted machine gun on the deck overlooking the garage. The felons must have figured out what was going on in the rec room and stationed themselves to ambush the agents as they emerged from the garage. Travis was too far away to get a good shot at them. All he succeeded in doing was attracting the shooter's attention.

"Go!" Travis shouted, and pushed Leah ahead of him. "Run!" She started running and he took off after her. They fled the hail of bullets that bit into the trees around them and plowed the leaf litter. When she stumbled, he pulled her up and dragged her farther into the woods, running blindly, praying they wouldn't be struck by the bullets that continued to rain around them.

He didn't see the edge of the bluff until it was too late. One moment his booted foot struck dirt, the next the ground fell away beneath him. The last sound he remembered was Leah's anguished scream, echoing over and over as they fell.

Chapter Three

Leah had thought she was ready for death. In the past six months there had been times she had prayed to die. But falling off that cliff, gunfire echoing around her, the ground rushing up to meet her, she wanted only to live. Her hands bound behind her by the cuffs, she had only Travis's strong arms to save her as he wrapped himself around her. She buried her face against his chest and prayed wordlessly, eyes closed against the fate that awaited.

They hit the ground hard. Her head struck the dirt and she rolled, a sharp ache in her shoulder.

Stunned, she lay slumped against a tree trunk, aware of distant shouts overhead and the sound of the rushing creek below.

Travis! Frantic, she struggled to sit and looked around. He lay ten feet down the slope, his big body still, blood trickling from a cut on his forehead. Crawling, half sliding on the steep grade, she made her way to him. "Travis!" she called. She nudged him with the toe of her shoe. "Travis, wake up."

The shouts overhead grew louder. She looked up toward the house, but trees blocked her view. Had Duane and the others seen them fall? Would they come down here to look for them? She leaned down, her face close to his, so that she could smell the clean scent of his soap, mingled with the burned cordite from the weapon he had fired. "Travis, you have to wake up," she pleaded. "We have to get out of here before they find us." Duane would waste no time killing them, as she had seen him kill others before. She nudged him with her knee. "Travis, please!"

He groaned and rolled away from her, clutching his injured head.

She scooted after him. "We have to get out of here." She kept her voice low, fearful Duane and the others might hear. The shouts had died down, but maybe they were only saving their breath for the climb down.

He groaned again, but shoved himself into a sitting position and studied her, his gaze unfocused. "Leah? What happened?"

"Duane was shooting at us and we went over the cliff." She glanced up the slope again, expecting to see Duane or one of his thugs barreling toward them. "We have to get out of here before they come after us. Please, untie me." She half turned and angled her cuffed hands toward him. Her shoulder ached with every movement, but she couldn't worry about that now.

He frowned at her, his vision clearing. "I remember now," he muttered. Some of the hardness had returned to his gaze, and she knew he was recalling not just what had happened moments before, but the ugly history between them.

"Please cut me loose," she said. "I can't move in this rough terrain with my arms behind my back like this. I promise I won't try to run away." He was her best hope of finally escaping from Duane Braeswood and his ruthless gang.

Travis hesitated, then shifted to pull a multitool from a pouch on his belt and cut the flexcuff. She cried out in relief, then pain, as she brought her arms in front of her.

"You're hurt." He was on his knees in front of her, concern breaking through the coldness in his expression. "Were you hit, or did it happen in the fall?"

"I landed on my shoulder." She rubbed the

aching joint. "I'm just a little banged up. But you took a nasty blow to the head. You're still bleeding."

She reached toward the gash on his forehead. He shied away from her touch. "I'm okay," He shoved to his feet, stumbling a little as he fought for balance. "Where are we?"

"Above the creek that runs below the house."

"Which direction is the road?" he asked.

"That way, I think." She pointed to their left.

"What's in the other directions?" he asked.

She tried to visualize the area, but in the two weeks since they had relocated here, she had spent most of her time in the house, or running errands in Durango. Duane never left her alone, and he would have laughed in her face if she had expressed a desire to hike in the woods behind the house, though she had grown up hiking and camping very near here. "I'm not sure. It's pretty rugged country. Duane had a map in his office of the Weminuche Wilderness area, so I think we're very near there."

"So no houses or roads?"

She shook her head. "Maybe some hiking trails, but nothing else. Wilderness is, well, wild. Undeveloped."

A gust of wind stirred the aspens, and a tree branch popped, making her jump. "We have to get out of here before they come after us," she said.

"Why wouldn't they be more interested in going after the rest of the team?" he asked, even as he ejected the magazine from his gun and shoved in a fresh one. "They don't even know who I am."

"They'll have figured out I'm with you." She stood and brushed dry leaves from her jeans. "Duane won't let me get away."

"Because you mean so much to him." No missing the bitterness behind those words.

"Because I know a lot about the things he's done and I can testify against him." And because he never let anyone cross him without making sure they paid for their betrayal. She started to move past him, but he snagged her arm.

"We're not leaving," Travis said. "We're going back up there."

She stared at him. "We can't go back. They'll kill us."

"I'm not leaving until I'm sure the rest of the team is all right." He holstered his weapon again and started up the slope, tugging her with him.

She gazed longingly down the slope toward the creek. "Try to run and I'll shoot you," he said.

The hardness of the words sent a chill through her. She could scarcely believe this was the same man who had once treated her with such tenderness. She couldn't blame him for hating her, though he would never understand how much she had suffered, too.

They scrambled up the slope, on their hands and knees at times. As they neared the top, he angled off to the side, and she realized he intended to approach the house obliquely. If they were very lucky, Duane or one of his men wouldn't be waiting for them at the top.

When they were almost to the top, he looked back at her. "Stay down," he said. "Don't come up until I tell you."

She wished she had a weapon, to defend herself and to help defend him. But he would never believe that was all she intended. "Be careful," she called after him as he completed the climb to the top, but he gave no indication that he had heard her.

She pressed her body to the ground, willing herself to be invisible and trying to hear what was happening above her. But the only sounds were the rustling of aspen leaves, the flutter of birds in the branches and the constant rush of the creek. A chill from the cold ground seeped into her, making her shiver. She had dressed casually for her shopping trip in town, in jeans and hiking boots and a light sweater, an outfit suitable for hitting the grocery store or the mall, but not for tramping around outdoors, where the fall air held a definite bite.

She wished she had warned Travis about the cameras Duane had positioned all around the house, so that when he was inside he could see anyone who approached from any angle. She should have told him about the two guns Duane carried at all times, and about the razor-sharp knife in his boot. She had seen him cut a man's throat with that knife once, an image that still haunted her nightmares.

Falling rocks and dirt alerted her to someone's approach. Relief surged through her when she recognized Travis returning. He scrambled down toward her, moving quickly. "The others are gone," he said. "Come on. We've got to get to the road and meet them."

She hurried to follow him, slipping in the loose dirt and leaf mold, scraping her hands on rocks. Two-thirds of the way to the creek, he stopped against a tree, both hands searching in his pockets. "I can't find my phone," he said.

"Maybe you lost it in the fall." She leaned against the same tree, a smooth-barked aspen, and tried to catch her breath.

He looked around, then began making his way across the slope, in the general direction of their original landing place. "Help me look," he said. "I've got to call the team and let them know to wait for us."

She followed him, scanning the ground around them, then dropping to her knees to feel about in the dried leaves and loose rocks. "It's not here," she said.

"It has to be here," He glared at the ground, as if the force of his anger could summon the phone. He turned to her. "Give me yours, then."

"I don't have a phone,"

"Don't lie to me. You always have your phone with you."

The woman he had known had always carried her phone with her, but she was a different person now. "Duane didn't allow me to have a phone," she said.

His brow furrowed, as if he hadn't understood her words, but before he could reply, a shout disturbed the woodland peace. "They're down here!" a man yelled, and a bullet sent splinters flying from a tree beside her head.

Travis launched himself at her, pushing her aside and rolling with her, down the slope toward the creek. He managed to stop them before they hit the water, then pulled her upright and began running along the creek bank. "Is the road this way?" he asked.

"I think so." She had a dim memory of a bridge over the creek a mile or so from the house.

Crashing noises and falling rock telegraphed their pursuer's approach. Travis took cover behind a broad-trunked juniper and drew his weapon, but after a moment he lowered the gun. "I can't get a clear shot and there's no sense letting them know for sure where we are. Come on." He tugged her after him once more.

"How do you know your friends will be waiting for us?" she asked as she struggled to keep up with him.

"If they aren't, we can flag down someone else to help," he said.

No sense pointing out that the road leading into the private neighborhood of mostly vacation homes didn't receive a lot of traffic, especially on a fall weekday. If they could avoid Duane and his men, the road did seem the best route for escape. Maybe the only route.

She didn't know how long they ran, climbing over rocks and skirting thick groves of aspens and scrub oak. They splashed through the icy water of the creek, soaking her shoes and her jeans to the knees, and crawled up the muddy creek bank. Her shoulder ached with every movement and she panted from the exertion, but still the road eluded them. She needed to stop and rest, but they couldn't afford to give their pursuers any opportunity to overtake them.

"There's the bridge, up ahead," Travis said, and she wanted to weep with relief.

"Are your friends waiting for us?" she asked.

"I can't see yet." He stopped, bent over with his hands on his knees, panting. Mud streaked his face and arms, and his pants, like hers, were wet almost to the knees. Blood matted his hair and had dried on his face, yet he was still the handsomest man she had ever known. She had been attracted to the tall, broad-shouldered Texan from the moment they met, in the halls of the San Antonio high school where she was a new student. Though they had gone their separate ways in college, they had stayed in touch, and when they both ended up living and working in Washington, DC, they had begun dating. She had been sure they had been on their way to a happily-ever-after, but Duane's arrival in her life had changed all that.

"I'm going up to take a look," Travis said, straightening. "When I give you the signal, come on up. And don't try anything. I'll have my gun on you."

He had added that last warning to deliberately hurt her, she was sure. "I told you, I won't try to run away," she said.

"Yeah, well, you've lied to me before."

He began climbing the bank. When he was halfway up, the roar of a powerful engine and the crunch of tires on gravel announced a vehicle's arrival. It stopped on the bridge and car doors slammed. Travis moved faster, probably eager to greet his friends.

She saw the danger before he did, the familiar pale face with the hawk nose and the thinning dark hair combed over, dark eyes peering out from beneath heavy brows. Duane didn't see her, focused instead on the man scaling the bank. Fear strangling her, she watched as he pulled a gun from inside his coat and took aim.

"Travis, run!" The scream ripped from her throat, and she lunged toward him as the blast of the gun shattered the woodland stillness.

Chapter Four

Leah's scream propelled Travis to one side, so that the bullet tore through his shirt, grazing his ribs. Pain momentarily blinded him as he rolled toward the creek, landing with a splash in the icy water. More shots hit the water around him until he reached the shelter of the bridge. Plastered against the concrete piling, he waited for more gunfire or for the shooter to climb down after him.

The expected hail of bullets came, but this time the shots weren't intended for him. The shooter had turned his attention to Leah, who huddled behind the thick-trunked juniper as the gunfire tore at the bark. The sight of her trapped that way drove Travis to act on raw instinct. He pushed himself away from the bridge piling, deliberately exposing himself to the shooter above. "Over here!" he shouted, and fired three shots in rapid succession.

When the shooter turned his attention to Travis, Leah ran. But not, as he had hoped, away from danger, but toward it. She catapulted toward him, slamming into him and driving him farther under the bridge. He wrapped his free arm around her and sheltered her between his body and the bridge piling. "Why didn't you leave when you had the chance?" he muttered.

"I told you I wouldn't leave." She touched his torn shirt. "You're hit. You're bleeding."

He pushed her hand away. "Nothing serious." Though he could feel blood seeping from the wound. "How many of them are there?" he asked.

"It depends if Duane left someone back at the house," she said. "There are four altogether—Duane, Eddie and two who just arrived yesterday, Buck and Sam. I never heard their last names. But I don't think Duane would have wanted to leave the house unguarded, so he probably left Sam there."

"Why Sam?"

"I overheard Eddie teasing him about not being a good shot. His specialty is technology." She glanced over her shoulder. "They'll come down the bank in a minute," she said.

"I'll kill them when they do." He readied the gun to fire.

"They'll wait until you run out of ammunition. They won't give up."

A rock tumbled down from the road, gathering momentum as it rolled, landing with a splash in the water. "They're coming down," she said, and buried her face against his chest.

He inhaled deeply, making himself go still. He had to shove aside the fear and call on all his strength. He had no control over what Duane and his thugs did, but he was in charge of his own actions. He raised the Glock and lined up the sights on where he thought the shooter would show himself, then took another breath and let it out slowly.

The echo of the gunshot against the concrete of the bridge made his ears ring, but the sight of the shooter staggering backward let him know he had done some damage. He had no time to bask in this victory, as a second man followed the first, this one armed with a shotgun capable of gutting them both with one shot. Travis retreated farther behind the bridge support, pulling Leah with him.

"We're going to have to run for it," he whispered, his mouth so close he was almost kissing her ear.

She stiffened. "That's crazy."

"Crazy enough to work. And it's our only chance." Already, he could hear someone moving down the other side of the bridge. "Climb onto my back and hang on tight," he said. "If I go down, keep running on your own, but until then, don't let go."

"I'll slow you down," she said. "Leave me here. I'm the one they want, anyway."

He was no longer certain of her relationship to Duane, but he wasn't going to let her go back to that killer. "You're still my prisoner," he said. "I'm not going to give you up to him." He slipped the revolver from the ankle holster, then turned his back to her. "Climb on. Keep your head down."

She jumped onto his back, her arms around his neck, her legs wrapped around his waist.

The weight was awkward, but not impossible. "When I give the word, scream as loud as you can," he said.

"Why?"

"Just do it. Scream as if you just saw the biggest, nastiest-looking spider you can imagine." She had always been terrified of spiders.

"All right."

The revolver in one hand, the Glock in the other, he watched the bank to his left. When a second shooter dropped into position there, Travis said, "Now!" and charged forward.

The keening wail she let loose echoed beneath the bridge, a high, sharp note that pierced his ears, but as he had hoped, the sound startled the two shooters as well. They hesitated a fraction of a second, long enough for Travis to gain the advantage. He charged toward the downstream shooter, both guns blazing. The man fell back.

At the same time, the upstream man couldn't risk firing, for fear of hitting his boss.

He stuck to the bank at the edge of the water, feet sinking deep in the gravel and mud, staggering as if fighting his way through molasses. Leah had fallen silent, her face pressed against his neck, her fingers digging into his shoulder. He turned to fire at the men, then pulled at her legs. "Can you run?" he asked.

"Yes." She nodded, her hair falling forward to obscure her face.

"Then we're going to run, as fast and as far as we can."

She was swifter than he would have expected, keeping pace with him as they zigzagged through the trees. He led the way up a slope away from the creek, deeper into the area she had identified as wilderness. The shooters had run after them, but they were slower and clumsier, stopping from time to time to fire in Travis and Leah's general direction. After what could have been a half an hour or only ten minutes, the sounds of the gunfire and their pursuers' shouted curses faded away.

Travis risked stopping near a downed pine tree. Leah collapsed onto the fallen trunk, holding her side and gasping for breath. Several moments passed before either of them spoke. "I've never been so terrified in my life," she said.

He holstered his weapon and sank down beside her. "I think we've lost them for now."

She shook her head. "Maybe. But they'll be back. They'll hunt us down."

"How can you be so sure?" She talked as if she knew these men so well, but how could that be, when she had only been with them a few months? He had known her for years and would have sworn he knew everything about her, and yet he had never seen her betrayal coming.

"They're ruthless," she said. "When Duane

decides he wants something, he'll stop at nothing to get it. He'll steal, kill and use people every way you can imagine. He's an expert at it." The grief that transformed her face as she spoke made him want to pull her to him, to comfort her. But he held back.

Instead, he looked around them, at the trees crowded so close together there was scarcely room to walk. The sky showed only in scattered puzzle pieces of pale blue between the treetops. He thought the creek was somewhere to their right, but he couldn't be sure, having lost his bearings in their frantic flight. "Do you have any idea where we are?" he asked.

She shook her head. "I've never had much of a sense of direction, remember?"

He almost smiled, remembering. Her propensity for getting turned around and lost had been one of their private jokes. At the entrance to a mall department store she would address him with mock seriousness. "I'm going in, but if I don't come out in an hour, you'll have to come in after me."

That particular trait of hers wasn't so funny right now. "Let's hope Duane and his gang don't know where we are, either." He stood and offered her his hand. "It's going to be dark in a few hours. We need to find a safe place to spend the night, but before that, we need to get back to the creek. Without water, we won't make it out here very long."

"Then what?" she asked.

"Then we have to find our way out of here, back to civilization and a phone." And they had to do it while avoiding the men who were out to kill them.

WITH NO WATCH or phone to consult for the time, Leah had no idea how long it took them to locate the creek. But by the time they stumbled and slid down the bank to the narrow stream, she was exhausted and thirsty enough that she was tempted to simply stretch out in the icy water and let it wash into her mouth.

But common sense—or maybe simply an overwhelming desire to stay strong enough to get out of here alive—stopped her. She grabbed hold of Travis's arm to stop him as he knelt at the water's edge. "We have to boil the water before we drink it," she said.

Hair tousled, face streaked with mud and blood, he looked like a man who had survived a street brawl. "How are we supposed to do that? And why?" He looked around. "I don't see any factories or even houses around here."

"The water is full of giardia—a little bug that will make you very, very sick. I had it once at summer camp and I know I never want to be that ill again. If we boil the water or treat it somehow, it will kill the parasite."

He sat back on his heels and scanned the bank around them. "There's plenty of fuel. I don't suppose you've taken up smoking since we last met?"

"No." She scanned the area, then looked back at him. "What kind of supplies do you have on you, besides your gun and ammunition and that multi-tool you used to cut off my flex-cuff?"

He hesitated, then emptied his pockets onto the ground between them—a wallet with his ID, a few credit cards and some cash; badge; the multi-tool; and the Glock and a magazine with ten bullets, plus an empty magazine. The revolver and half a dozen bullets for it. A Mini Maglite, a small notebook and the binoculars. Her mood lifted when she spotted the Maglite. "We can use this," she said. "Now all we need is something to boil the water in. Look around for a tin can."

"We're in the wilderness," he reminded her, as he refilled his pockets.

"Trash washes downstream from other places," she said. "And it lasts a long time in this dry climate." Already, she was headed upstream, studying the bank.

Fifteen minutes later, she had almost given up when she spotted the soda can wedged in the roots of a wild plum growing along the banks. She crawled down and retrieved the can, then stopped to pick the few withered and spotted fruits left in the almost-leafless branches. She hurried with her finds downstream, where Travis was studying a deep pool. "There's fish in here, if I could figure out how to catch them," he said.

"Good idea." She held up the soda can. "If you cut the top off of this with your multi-tool, we can use it to heat water."

"Did you find matches, too?" he asked, taking the can.

She grinned. "I still remember a few lessons from playing around in the woods as a kid," she said.

While he cut the top from the soda can and straightened out the dents, she gathered dry pine needles and twigs. Atop these, she added shredded paper from his notebook. Then she pulled a pack of gum from her pocket. "What are you going to do with that?" he asked.

"You'll see." She unwrapped the gum and offered him the stick. He took it and popped it into his mouth, then she carefully tore the wrapper in half lengthwise, then pinched off bits out of the middle until only a thin sliver of paper-backed foil connected the two wider halves. "Now I need the battery from the Maglite," she said.

He unscrewed the bottom from the Maglite and shook out the battery. "I see where you're going with this, I think," he said. "You're going to make a spark."

"You got it." Gingerly, she pressed one end of the gum wrapper, foil side down, against the negative end of the battery. "This is the tricky part," she said. "I don't want to get burned." Holding her breath, she touched the other end of the foil to the positive end of the battery. Immediately the center of the foil began to brown and char, then burst into flame. She dropped the burning wrapper onto the tinder she had prepared, and it flared also. As the twigs caught, she began feeding larger pieces of wood onto it.

"Where did you learn that?" Travis asked.

"My best friend's older brother showed us when we were kids. He accidentally set the woods behind his house on fire doing that one time, but mostly we just thought it was a neat way to start campfires. I haven't thought of it in

years." She looked around. "I think we're ready
for the water now."

"I'll get it." He returned a few minutes later,
carrying the first can, along with a second. "I
found this," he said. "We can heat twice as much
water."

He nestled the water-filled cans among the
flames. The metal blackened and the water
began to steam. Several minutes later, it was
boiling. "It needs to boil ten minutes," she said.
"We'll have to guess how long that is." She
took one of the dried plums from her pockets.
"I found these. If we cut off the bad spots, they
should be okay to eat."

"I have to have water before I can eat anything," he said. "But we'll try them later. I had
no idea you were so resourceful in the wilderness."

"I told you my family spent a lot of time camping when I was a kid. We lived not that far from here before we moved to Texas."

"Where you acted like just another music-listening, mall-going city kid," he said.

"I was a teenager. I wanted to fit in." Most of all, she had wanted to impress him—and he had seemed so sophisticated and cool. Or at least, as sophisticated and cool as a sixteen-year-old could be. Back then, she wouldn't have admitted to knowing how to start a campfire or forage for wild food for anything.

"Did Braeswood know you were from around here?"

She focused on the boiling water, though she could feel his gaze burning into her. No matter how she tried to explain her relationship with Duane to Travis, he would never believe her. He had made up his mind about her the day she betrayed him. She didn't blame him for his anger, but she wasn't going to waste her breath defending herself. "He knew," she said. She had been shocked to discover how much Duane already knew about her when they met. But that was how he worked. He mined information the way some men mine gold or diamonds, and then he used that information to buy what he wanted.

Travis shifted and winced. Guilt rushed over her. "I forgot all about your wound," she said. "How is it?"

"It's no big deal." He started to turn away, but she leaned over to touch his wrist.

"Let me look," she said. "Now that we have water, I can at least clean it up."

He hesitated, then lifted his shirt to show an angry red graze along the side of his ribs. Now it was her turn to wince. "That must hurt," she said.

"I've felt better."

She glanced back at the water. "Where's that

handkerchief you were using to gag me?" she asked.

He pulled it from the pocket of the cargo pants.

Carefully, she dipped one corner of the cloth into the boiling water, took it out and let it cool slightly, then began sponging at the wound. "It doesn't look too deep," she said. She tried not to apply too much pressure, but she felt him tense when she hit a sensitive spot. As she cleared away the blood and dirt, she became aware of the smooth, taut skin beneath her hand. He had the muscular abs and chest of a man who worked out—abs and chest she had fond memories of feeling against her own naked body.

"I think it's clean enough now," he said, pulling away and lowering the shirt with a suddenness that made her wonder if he had read her thoughts.

She handed him the handkerchief. "You can clean that in the creek," she said. "The water has probably boiled enough. If we put it in the creek, it will cool down faster." She pulled the sleeves of her sweater down over her hands, intending to use them to protect her hands from the hot metal.

"I'll get that," he said, and lifted first one can, then the other, off the fire with the pliers from his multi-tool.

She followed him to the creek, where they waited while the water steamed in the cans. "As soon as we drink these, we should heat more," she said. "And try to find some food."

"I'm not comfortable spending the night by the creek," he said. "If Braeswood and his men are hunting for us, they'll know we have to have water. How well does he know the area?"

"He knows it pretty well." She closed her eyes, picturing the maps of the Weminuche Wilderness he had taped to the walls of the room he used as his office. When she opened them, she found herself looking right into Travis's blue eyes. That intense gaze—and the mistrust she saw there—made her feel weighted down and more exhausted than ever. "He had maps of the area," she said. "He planned to escape through the wilderness if the Feds trapped him at the house."

"Why did he come back when he did?" Travis asked. "We should have had plenty of time to search the place and get out before any of you returned from Durango."

"The neighbor, Mr. Samuelson, called Duane. He said some utility workers were up at the house, but they looked suspicious. Duane had made a point of making friends with the old man. He asked him to report if he saw any strangers around the house. He used the excuse that he had a lot of valuables that burglars would want. After he got off the phone with Samuelson, Duane called my driver, Preston Wylie, and told him to take me back to the house and he would be right behind me." If she and Wylie had reached the house first, she had considered asking the strangers, whoever they were, to take her with them. But she dismissed the idea almost as soon as it came to her. She knew Wylie had orders to kill her if she tried to get away. Duane almost never left her unguarded, but the few times he had risked it, he had made it very clear that he would hunt her down and kill her if she ever left him. He had the men and resources at his disposal to find her, probably before she had gotten out of the state. She had resigned herself to being trapped with him forever.

Then Travis, of all people, had pulled her from that car and risked his life to help her get away. Maybe he only saw it as protecting a prisoner, but the result was the same. No matter if he hated her, she would always be grateful to him for taking her away from an impossible situation.

"What can you remember about that escape route Braeswood had planned?" Travis asked. "Are there back roads or trails he intended to follow? A hideout where he thought he could hole up for a while?"

She shook her head. "I don't remember anything. I only saw the map a few times, and I didn't pay much attention to it then. He certainly didn't share his plans with me." If the time had come to flee the house, he would have assigned a guard to drag her along with them, one more piece of baggage he considered necessary, at least for the moment.

"I guess he didn't like to mix his personal relationship with his professional ones," Travis said.

"I think the water is cool enough to drink now." She ignored the gibe and plucked one of the cans from the stream and drained it. Even warm, it tasted so good going down. As soon as she had drained it, she refilled it and carried it back up to the fire. "I'm going to look for something to eat besides those plums," she said.

"I'll come with you." He added his refilled can to the fire and followed her.

"I told you, you don't have to worry about me running away," she said.

"Right now I'm more worried about you getting lost."

"I'll be okay, as long as I follow the creek."

He fell into step behind her. "What are we looking for?" he asked.

"Berries, cattails, more plum trees. There are edible mushrooms, but I don't know enough about them to risk it."

"If I had line and a hook, I could try fishing."

"We could try to make a string from grass or vines," she said. "And you could try my earring hooks."

"Maybe I'll give it a go later, after we've found a safe place to camp."

She paused beside a small shrub and began pulling off the bright red fruit. "What are those?" he asked.

"Rose hips." She bit into one and made a face. "They're supposed to be full of vitamin C. They taste pretty sour, but they're not the worst thing I ever ate."

He took one, bit into it, then spit it out. "I don't want to know the worst thing you ever ate."

In the end, she collected two more plums, a handful of rose hips and some wild onions. "I sure hope you can catch a fish," she said. "This isn't going to get us very far."

"I'm determined to find a way out of here long before we have to worry about starving," he said. "Let's go back and get the water, then find a place to stay tonight. Then we need to figure out a route away from here."

They headed back downstream. She smelled the smoke from their little fire long before they reached it. Not good, if Duane was tracking them. She hurried to retrieve the cans of boiling water and set them aside to cool. "We'll need to scatter these ashes and cover them with dirt, then leaves, to hide the fact that we were here," she said.

"I'll get a branch or something to dig with," Travis said, and moved off into the woods.

For the first time since they had stopped by the creek, Leah began to feel uneasy. They had remained in one place too long. It wouldn't be that difficult for Duane to follow the creek in the direction he knew they had fled. Another man might have left them to die in the wilderness, but Duane didn't take those kinds of chances. He was successful because he believed in controlling all variables. She was a variable he was most determined to control.

Footsteps behind her alerted her to Travis's return. "The water's cool enough to drink now," she said, gingerly picking up the still-warm can. "Let's empty them and take them with us."

Strong hands grabbed her roughly from behind. The can of water slipped from her grasp as she felt a sharp sting, and then the pressure of a razor-sharp blade held to her throat. Duane's gravelly voice whispered in her ear, "Where's your friend the FBI agent?"

Chapter Five

Travis fought his way through a tangle of vines and was reaching for a stout stick that might serve as a shovel when a strangled squeak made him freeze. It might have been the distress cry of a mouse or a bird, it was so faint, but instinct told him the noise came from Leah, and she was in trouble.

Carrying the stick like a club, he moved as swiftly and silently as he could back toward the campfire. His first view of the area was of Braeswood holding Leah, but this wasn't a loving embrace. Rage momentarily blinded him at the sight of the knife at her throat.

"I…I don't know," she stammered, in answer to something Braeswood said. "He was angry with me. He left."

"Liar!" Blood ran in a thin line down the pale column of her neck. Travis had to grab hold of a tree trunk to keep from lunging forward. Setting the stick carefully aside, he drew the Glock from the holster. All he needed was one clear shot.

"No sign of him, boss." One of the other men—probably Buck—joined Braeswood and Leah beside the smoldering fire.

"Where's Eddie?" Braeswood asked.

Buck made a face. "He'll be along in a minute. He's out of shape."

Duane unsnapped a radio from his belt. "Bobcat Two, do you read me?"

"I'm here, boss."

"Any sign of those Feds?"

"Negative."

"You got our location on GPS?"

"Yes, sir."

"Meet us at the pickup point in two hours with the rest of the team. We should be finished here by then."

"I'll be there."

Braeswood repocketed the radio. "By the time the Feds get back to the house, there won't be anything left for them to find. And we'll have taken care of Leah's friend."

"Maybe he really did leave her," Buck said.

"He was here." Braeswood nodded to the two cans of water nestled in the coals. "He probably went to get more wood or something."

"He's wounded," Leah said. "Why waste your time with him? He's just another dumb Fed. If you leave now, you'll be out of the country before anyone even knows."

"Shut up." Braeswood shook her. "Don't think

I won't kill you right now if you don't stop an-
noying me."

"Maybe I'd rather die than spend any more
time with you."

The crack of his palm striking her face echoed
through the trees. Her head snapped back and
she cried out again. Travis braced against a tree
trunk and sighted along the barrel of the Glock,
but Braeswood was still too close to her. Travis
needed a plan for dealing with the second thug,
too. And the third one who might arrive soon.

Leah moaned and slumped in Braeswood's
arms, body limp, eyes closed. The sudden weight
of her made him stagger back. He nudged her
shoulder with the butt of his gun. "Wake up. I
didn't hit you that hard."

A noise to their left, like a large animal stumbling through the underbrush, drew their attention. "That's probably Eddie," Buck said.

It probably was, Travis thought. But none of

them could see him yet, so he saw his chance. "Luke!" He shouted the name of his fellow team member. "Over here!"

The others froze, long enough for Travis to get off a good shot at Buck, who staggered, then dropped to his knees and toppled over, blood spreading from the bullet hole in his chest. Travis turned his attention to Braeswood, who was struggling with Leah. She had come out of her stupor, which Travis suspected had been faked, and had taken advantage of the distraction to pull away from Braeswood. He still had hold of her arm, but he had dropped the knife, and she kicked and scratched at him, making it impossible for him to draw his gun.

"Braeswood, let her go." Travis stepped from the edge of the woods, his Glock leveled at the terrorist. Braeswood released Leah and went for his own weapon. She fled into the trees to their right.

Travis's first shot missed, as Braeswood dived behind a tree. He returned fire, bullets biting into the trees around Travis, forcing him to take cover also. A few seconds later, a second round of shots narrowly missed him. Eddie had arrived and was firing from behind a fallen pine.

Travis flattened himself in a dip in the ground and debated his next move. He had maybe half a dozen bullets left for the Glock, and a few for the revolver. Not enough to outlast these two. And Leah was out there somewhere, running. If he made a mistake and ended up getting killed, she would be alone, with Braeswood and his men after her.

Stealthily, he began crawling backward through the underbrush. When he judged he was out of sight of Braeswood and Eddie, he stood and ran, choosing a course he hoped would intersect the one Leah had taken.

He heard her long before he saw her, crashing through the woods like an animal fleeing in panic. He increased his own pace and waited until he spotted the bright red of her sweater before he called out. "Leah! It's me, Travis. Wait up!"

She darted behind a tree, then peered out cautiously at him. Tears streaked her face, and her lip was swollen where Braeswood had hit her. When Travis reached her, he pulled her close, crushing her to him. Seeing Braeswood strike her had destroyed his determination to keep some physical distance between them. "Are you all right?" he asked.

She nodded, her face pressed against his shoulder. The subtle floral scent of her perfume tickled his senses, stirring emotions he wasn't ready to examine too closely. "I'm okay," she said, out of breath. "Scared. A little shaken. But okay. What about you?"

The concern in her eyes when she lifted her

head to look at him made him tighten his hold
on her. "I'm okay." Though the memory of her
with that knife to her throat would haunt him
for a long time to come.

She jerked in his arms as a crack, like a stick
snapping underfoot, sounded in the distance.
"They're coming after us," she said, panic wid-
ening her eyes. "I told you, he won't give up."

"We've got to keep moving." He took her hand
and led the way, moving as fast as they could
in the dense forest, following animal trails and
the paths of old fires, uncertain of the direction
they were traveling. Was it true that people who
were lost in the woods tended to walk in circles?
Did that mean they could end up accidentally
stumbling into Braeswood and the others?

Leah tripped on a tree root and went flying,
landing on her hands and knees in the dirt. "I
can't keep doing this," she said as Travis helped
her up. "I'm too exhausted."

Before long, he would be too worn out to go much farther, as well. His side where he had been shot and his head where he had fallen earlier both throbbed, and he had noticed Leah wincing every time she moved her shoulder. He had been betting they could outlast Braeswood and his men, but maybe that had been foolish thinking. The hatred or greed or whatever force that motivated the terrorist was a powerful driver. "We'll have to find a place to hide," he said.

She nodded and closed her eyes, struggling to catch her breath.

He scanned the ground around them and spotted a dead pine tree, uprooted in some past storm. The roots stretched into the air above the hole where they had once been planted. "Over here," he said, and led her to the hole. It was large enough to accommodate two people. He helped Leah down into the depression, then dragged a tangle of branches and vines over it. After scattering leaves to hide their footsteps, he slipped into the hole behind her and tugged the last branch into place.

"Do you really think they won't see us?" she asked.

"We'll see them first." He grasped the Glock and peered out of their makeshift shelter. If Braeswood or one of his men did try to attack them here, Travis would have the first chance to get off a good shot.

Minutes passed, their breathing growing more regular and even. Then the unmistakable sound of footsteps on the forest floor grew louder. Leah clutched at him, but said nothing. Seconds later, Eddie Roland appeared, followed closely by Braeswood. Both men were armed—Braeswood with his pistol, while Eddie had traded his handgun for a semiautomatic rifle. The two men moved deliberately, studying the ground around them.

"I know they came this way," Braeswood said. "I saw their tracks."

"It's hard to follow anything in this heavy underbrush," Roland said. "We need a dog. They can track anything."

"We don't have a dog, idiot," Braeswood said. "They can't have gotten far. The only place Leah ever walked was on a treadmill."

At the mention of her name, she pressed her face more firmly against Travis's chest. Her silken hair tickled his chin, the sensation at once foreign and achingly familiar. In the silence while the two men above them searched, he became aware of her heartbeat, strong and rapid against his own.

After a while, he couldn't hear their two pursuers anymore. "I think they've moved on," he whispered.

"We should wait in case they come back," she said.

"We will." He settled more comfortably into the bottom of the hole, though he kept his eyes trained on the opening above them, and his ears attuned for any sound of approach. "Try to get some rest," he said softly. "I'll keep watch."

"I'll watch with you," she said, but within moments he felt the tension drain from her body and her breathing grow more even. The physical and emotional stress of the last few hours had taken their toll.

Determined to stay awake, he turned his mind to analyzing the day's events. He had arrived at the log home where Braeswood and his team were hiding with a clear idea of his mission. His job was to capture and arrest a group of terrorists. One of those terrorists happened to be his ex-fiancée, but that didn't make her less guilty of the horrible crimes the group was responsible for.

Now, after a few hours with Leah, he was less sure of the latter. Seeing how afraid she was of Braeswood, and how cruelly he treated her, Travis was beginning to doubt she had gone with the man willingly. He had believed she left him because she had fallen in love with someone else—what else could "changed my mind" have meant? Later, when he had learned she was living with Braeswood, he was shocked and angered that the woman he had loved and trusted had left him for a murderer.

But he had sensed no love between Leah and the terrorist leader when he saw them together now, only fear. Braeswood had clearly been intent on killing her once he used her to lure in Travis.

So why had she left Travis for a man who only seemed to want to harm her? Before this ordeal was over, he intended to know the answer to that question.

An hour or more had passed when she stirred awake. She sat up, blinking. "I didn't mean to fall asleep," she said, pushing her hair out of her eyes.

"It made sense for you to rest while you had the chance." He checked the view through the narrow opening. Long shadows stretched across the ground, telling him the sun would be setting soon. "Are you ready to head out again?" he asked.

"I guess so. I'm so thirsty." She rubbed her stomach. "And hungry, too."

"We're going to do something about that," he said.

"What?"

"We have to go back to the area where we had the fire, near the creek."

Fear tightened her features. "If Duane retraces his path, he'll find us."

"We have to take that chance." He stood and pushed aside branches to widen the opening to their shelter, then pulled her to her feet.

"Why?" she asked.

"They didn't have Buck or his pack with them when they moved past, so they must have left him there. He had at least one water bottle in that pack, and probably food and other supplies. And he probably has a phone we can use to call for help."

Her expression grew more animated at this news. "I hadn't thought of that. Then yes, we should definitely go back." She started to haul herself out of the hole, but he pulled her back.

"Let me go first."

"Why? So they can shoot you in the head first? At least you can cover me. Don't count on me for the same."

"I can pull you up to the ground," he said.

"You can boost me up from here."

"Are you always this stubborn?"

She smiled. "Always."

Something broke inside him at that remark, some last restraint against his emotions. Not thinking, he pulled her close and looked into her eyes. "I've missed you," he said, his voice rough with emotion.

"I've missed you, too." She brushed her hand along his cheek, then leaned in to bring her lips to his, gently at first, then hungrily, as if he were all the food and drink she craved.

He responded in kind, all the anxiety and anger and despair of their months apart channeled into that kiss. He still didn't know what to think about her betrayal, and he wasn't ready to trust her, but for this moment, stranded with only each other to depend on, he gave in to the need to simply be close to her. To be with her, emotionally, in a way he had never allowed himself to be with any other person.

She pulled away first and regarded him with an expression he read as equal parts wariness and hope. "Does this mean you've forgiven me?" she asked.

"No." He touched the corner of her mouth, which was still swollen from Braeswood's blow. "But I'm not blaming you the way I once did. Consider it a first step in a long journey."

She pulled away. "Speaking of long journeys, we'd better get going."

He checked the opening, and seeing nothing but still woodland, he boosted her up, then climbed out himself. "Do you know the way back to the body?" she asked.

"I think so," he said.

In the end, they were able to follow Braeswood's and Roland's tracks through the woods. The two men hadn't been concerned about being followed, and their heavy boots and careless steps made a trail of scuffed leaves, broken branches and even boot prints that led all the way to the little clearing, where the remains of the campfire still smoldered, and one of the cans of water sat, undisturbed, Buck's body slumped a few yards away.

Leah hurried to retrieve the can of water. She drank half and handed the rest to Travis . "You take it," he said, returning the can. "I'll get the bottle on Buck's pack."

Already, the body was drawing flies. Travis ignored them and focused on unbuckling the pack from the dead man's back. He set it aside, then riffled through Buck's pockets. He found a wallet with three different driver's licenses, identifying him variously as Bradley Simons, Brent Sampson and Bartholomew Spietzer. He had a couple of credit cards and twenty-three dollars in cash. Travis replaced the wallet and riffled through his other pockets, coming up with a pack of breath mints, some change, a Ruger .45-caliber pistol and an extra clip of ammo, and finally, in his front jeans pocket, a cell phone.

"He has a phone," he said.

Leah knelt a short distance away. "Can you call someone to come and get us?"

He tapped the phone to waken it, relieved to discover Buck hadn't bothered locking it, then punched in the direct number to his supervisor, Special Agent in Charge Ted Blessing. The screen almost immediately went black. He frowned and checked the display again. "We don't have a signal," he said.

Leah sat back on her heels. "I should have thought of that," she said. "Wilderness areas don't have cell towers. Plus all these trees..." She tilted her head back to regard the pines and firs that towered overhead.

"Maybe we can climb to a better signal." He pulled the water bottle from the pack and drank deeply, then offered some to her.

She shook her head. "I'm okay. But I'd like to know if there's any food in there."

"We should move to a safer location before we check it out," he said. He stood and shouldered the pack. "Whatever is in here, it's heavy enough." Anything they didn't absolutely need, he would discard at the first opportunity. They had to move quickly, and that meant not taking anything that would weigh them down.

He led the way back into deeper woods—not taking the path they had followed to get here, but moving, he hoped, closer to the road. Leah followed, saying nothing. After a while, he noticed she still carried the two empty soda cans. "We might need them," she said when she saw him looking at them.

"Good idea." She had come up with a lot of

good ideas so far during this ordeal. Another civilian might have been a burden, but she was turning out to be a capable partner. As much as he had loved her before, he wasn't sure he had ever respected her the way he did now.

Chapter Six

It was almost dark before Travis felt it was safe enough for them to stop moving. He had held out the hope of making it to the road before they halted, but navigating among the trees grew dangerous as the darkness deepened. He halted in a small clearing backed by a shelf of rock. "We can't go any farther without light," he said. "And I don't want to risk using the flashlight, in case the wrong people spot it." He didn't bring up the worry that Braeswood and his men might have night-vision goggles or infrared scanners, which would make finding them much easier.

"No, we won't risk it." Leah sank to the ground. Her shoulders slumped and her face was slack with exhaustion.

"Are you okay?" he asked.

She straightened and looked up at him, forcing a smile. "I'm fine. And I'm anxious to see what's in that pack. If we shield the flashlight with our bodies, we can risk taking a look. I'm hoping for food." She rubbed her arms against the night chill. "And maybe a fleece jacket."

Travis slung the pack from his shoulder and dropped it onto the ground in front of her. Then he lowered himself to sit beside her, their shoulders almost touching. He switched on the Mini Maglite and propped it against a couple of rocks so that the beam shone on the pack. Then he opened the top of the backpack and began laying out its contents. First out was a wrinkled black fleece jacket. He handed it to Leah and she immediately wrapped it around her shoulders. "Not only will it keep you warm, it will make you tougher to spot," he said.

She smoothed her hand over the sleeve of her red sweater. "I wasn't anticipating having to flee through the woods when I got dressed this morning."

"Where were you going when you first left the house?" he asked.

"I had an appointment for a manicure." She studied her chipped nail polish.

"How nice for you."

She glared at him. "It was better than being stuck alone with my jailers all the time."

Now would probably be a good time for him to ask her more about her time with Duane, and how she had ended up with the man in the first place. The more time he spent with her, the harder it was to think of her as a terrorist. But he wasn't ready to let down his guard with her yet. And how would he know she wasn't telling him more lies? Better to put off finding out a little longer.

He returned his attention to the pack and pulled out two sandwiches. He sniffed the packets. "Peanut butter and jelly," he said, and handed her one.

"My favorite," she said. "At least right now it is." She tore open the plastic zipper bag.

He unwrapped the second sandwich and took a bite. Rich peanut butter and strawberry jam on wheat bread—it wasn't steak, but he was definitely going to savor it. Sandwich in one hand, he dug with the other into the pack again. He pulled out a water filter. "That should come in handy." He realized why the pack had been so heavy as it continued to yield treasures: a first aid kit, protein bars, two more clips of .45-caliber ammo, a Mylar space blanket, a plastic garbage bag, matches and cotton wool for starting fires, and another bottle of water. In a side pocket of the bag he found a headlamp and a map and compass. Tension he hadn't even realized he had been holding went out of him. "With these we should be able to find our way out of here," he said.

"Hmmm." Leah had opened the first aid kit and was riffling through it. "Looks like Buck was pretty well prepared. There's all kinds of meds and bandages here." She stopped, and a faint blush edged up her cheeks, visible even in the flashlight's glow.

"What is it?" Travis leaned toward her to see what had caught her attention.

She held up a familiar foil packet, the kind used for condoms. "Like I said, Buck was prepared for anything."

He choked off a laugh, disguising it as a cough. He began putting everything back in the pack. "It's getting dark. We need to make a shelter for the night."

"It's getting colder, too." She wrapped her arms around herself. "We've been having frost at night."

"If we can make a kind of lean-to with branches, it will help hide us and block any wind." He stood and shouldered the pack. "We can wrap up in the space blanket and we should be all right." He grabbed the flashlight. "Help me find some branches."

AS LEAH HELPED Travis cut and tear branches from nearby spruce trees, he talked about his plans for the morning. "We'll get an early start, refill both water bottles, then climb until we get cell service," he said. "If we can get above the trees, we should be able to figure out where we are, now that we have a map. The Bureau might even be able to get a helicopter in here to retrieve us."

He made it all sound so easy, but all she could

think was *We have to get through the night first.* She wasn't as afraid of Duane as she had been. The sight of Buck lying dead had calmed her, in a way. It had shown her that despite his power, Duane wasn't invincible. Now that Travis had more ammunition and another gun, she believed the two of them had a chance of outrunning and outwitting Duane.

Her uneasiness now all centered on the prospect of spending the long, dark hours in close proximity to Travis. Though the kiss they had shared proved passion still sparked between them, she didn't believe he had really forgiven her. And she still had plenty of reasons for keeping some distance between them, no matter the temptation.

"Here. Take this." He handed her the flashlight and bent and gathered an armful of cut branches. She had put on Buck's jacket, rolling the too-long sleeves up over her wrists. Though the fleece smelled of stale cigarette smoke, she was grateful for its soft warmth as the night air chilled. "Shine the light over there by those rocks." Travis nodded to their right, and she did as he asked. A long-dead fir, the trunk bare of bark and stripped of limbs, lay on its side, the tip caught in the rocks. Travis moved to this area and began leaning the largest branches against the tree trunk. The result was a kind of tent made of soft fir boughs. He stepped back. "What do you think?"

"It looks…small."

"It will be easier to stay warm that way." He took off the pack, opened it, and removed the space blanket. "We'll spread this out to help block the cold from the ground, then wrap ourselves up in it. Here, take this end and crawl in."

She hesitated, but since her only other option was spending the night outside in freezing temperatures, she would have to make the best of it.

She crawled into the shelter, dragging the stiff, crackling foil-lined blanket with her. "What am I supposed to do now?" she called.

"Get comfortable, then I'll squeeze in beside you and we'll wrap the blanket around us."

She could have pointed out that on the cold ground in the dark woods, against hard rocks, wearing the same clothes she had had on all day, with no pillows or wine or chocolate or any of the indulgences she considered necessary, the probability of anything close to comfortable was less than zero. But pity parties were best celebrated solo, so she kept quiet. She arranged the blanket under her as best she could, settled her back against the rocks, and tried not to think of the bugs that were probably sharing this space with her. "Okay," she called.

He came sliding in, immediately shrinking the space to the size of a coffin. Unfortunate comparison, she thought. He grunted and turned on his side. "Does your side hurt where you were shot?" she asked, momentarily forgetting her own discomfort.

"It's okay. What about your shoulder and your neck?"

In the rush to escape Duane and everything that had happened since, she hadn't had much time to dwell on what had happened to her. "My shoulder is a little sore, but it will be all right," she said. She put a hand to her throat and felt the line of dried blood. "My neck doesn't hurt, but I hope I don't end up with some nasty infection."

"I can take care of that." He leaned forward and dragged the backpack, which he had left at his feet, up onto his legs. He fished out the head-lamp and the first aid kit. The light made a soft white glow in the shelter, illuminating his face and whatever he looked at. He opened a disinfecting wipe and dabbed gently at her neck. "This might sting a little."

It didn't sting. Or if it did, a little sting didn't have a chance to claim her attention, competing as it was with the hot flutterings of arousal that danced up and down her skin at his touch. Apparently satisfied that the wound was clean, he tucked the wipe into a pocket of the pack and took out a tube of antibiotic ointment and began dabbing it onto the cut. "I don't think we need to bandage it," he said. "He didn't go deep."

"He just wanted to scare me." Duane was an expert at that.

Travis's hand stilled and he looked down at her, though the light prevented her from seeing his expression. "You say that like it wasn't the first time," he said.

"It wasn't." She had spent most of her time with Duane in various stages of terror. It was how he operated. How he maintained control.

Travis busied himself putting away the first aid supplies, then shoved the pack to his feet

once more and switched off the light. He settled back against the rock, their bodies pressed
together all along that side, but desire had left
her, his silence a wall between them.

She didn't have the words to heal the wound
she had caused him, so she waited, letting the
night sounds fill the void: the rustle of wind in
the trees, the creak of a branch, the whisper of
some small creature in the leaf litter on the forest floor. Eyes closed, she breathed in deeply of
the Christmas-tree fragrance of the cut spruce,
and thought of the last Christmas she and
Travis had spent together. They had attended
the lighting of the National Christmas Tree on
the Ellipse, and later enjoyed a concert at the
National Cathedral. It had been the most magi-
cal holiday in her memory, his love the best gift
she could have ever received.

And three months later, it all ended. Duane
had stolen that magic from her, and as long as

she lived, she didn't think she would have it in her to forgive him for that.

"I've spent the past six months trying to make sense of what happened." Travis spoke softly, but she heard the anger and hurt behind the words.

"It's not something that makes sense," she said. "Not even to me, sometimes."

"I'm ready to listen."

"Are you?" She angled toward him, wishing she could see his face, but the darkness was too complete. She had only her awareness of him, of the broadness of his shoulders and the angle of his arm and the muscles of his thighs where he touched her.

"I saw you with Braeswood this afternoon," he said "You were afraid of him. And he didn't look at you with anything close to love."

"Oh, Duane doesn't love me. He doesn't love anyone but himself."

"Do you love him?" Travis asked.

"Never. I couldn't. I've seen him kill. I know how ruthless he can be."

"Your note to me said you had changed your mind. I thought you meant you found someone else. I believed all this time that you were in love with Braeswood."

"No." She felt in the darkness and found the back of his hand. When he tried to pull away, she laced her fingers with his and held on tight. "I lied. I didn't love anyone else. I don't love anyone else." Though if her feelings for Travis were still love after all that had happened, she couldn't say.

"Why did you lie?" He asked the question in the same tone he must use to interrogate a suspect. *Why did you kill that woman? Why did you swindle those people out of all that money? How could you pretend to justify your crime?*

She sighed and closed her eyes. What could

she say that would ever persuade him she wasn't lying now? All she had was the truth. "I didn't want you to come after me."

"Why not?"

"Because he would have killed you."

"Braeswood?"

"Yes." Duane had made her choice very clear—give up Travis, or he would be dead. Either way, she would lose him. Better to let him escape alive.

He rolled onto his side to face her. Their bodies were so close she could feel the heat of him, smell the sweat and spice fragrance of him. "But you said you didn't love him. Why did you go with him?"

"It's a long story." One she wasn't sure she could tell without breaking down.

"We've got all night."

Yes, and when she was done, he might hate

her even more. "I'll tell you, if you'll listen to everything before you judge," she said.

"I don't—"

He started to protest, but she put her fingers to his lips, silencing him. "I know you. You want to fix things. This isn't something you can fix."

"All right."

She moved down, the space blanket crackling under her, until she was flat on her back, staring up at the blackness, and prepared to relive a darkness far worse than the absence of light in this shelter.

"Hello?" Leah answered the phone that March afternoon over six months before with her usual efficiency. The display on her cell showed her sister Sarah's number. "Sarah, why didn't you call on the office phone? You know that's the best way to reach me during working hours." Her younger sister also worked in the

Senate Office Building, and the two often got together after work for drinks or to take in a movie. She glanced toward the open door into her boss's office as she answered her cell phone, but Senator Diana Wilson was engrossed in a phone call of her own.

"Leah, you've got to help." The words came out half choked, so unlike Sarah's usually cheery rush of conversation.

"Sarah? What's wrong? Why are you crying? What's happened?"

"Your sister is perfectly safe. For now." The man's voice on the other end of the line was calm. Too calm, almost like one of those robotic voices that gave directions on voice mail. "As long as you cooperate, she'll remain that way."

"What are you talking about? Who is this?"

"Keep your voice down, Leah. You don't want to upset the senator. Not if you want to see your sister alive again."

The words froze the blood in her veins. Panic squeezed her chest. She had to fight to breathe and couldn't speak. She glanced over her shoulder toward the senator's office again.

"Tell the senator you need to take off work a little early and come to the address I'm going to text you. Come alone. I promise your sister will be there and the two of you can talk."

"I don't understand," she whispered.

But the man had already hung up.

Shaking, she opened the bottom desk drawer and took out her purse, then staggered to the senator's door. Senator Wilson was still on a call, but she raised her eyebrows in question. "I…I'm not feeling very well," Leah said. "I think I need to go home."

Eyes full of concern, the senator nodded. "Take care," she mouthed, and waved Leah away.

She didn't remember leaving the building.

She was on her way to the metro station when her text notification signal chimed. The screen showed an address off Dupont Circle. Running now, Leah hurried to the metro station and caught a train just leaving that would take her to Dupont Circle.

Sarah answered the door to the basement apartment where Leah had been directed, but as soon as she had pulled Leah inside, a man she would soon come to know as Duane Braeswood, along with two other men, emerged from a back room, all three carrying guns.

Leah forced herself to be strong, for her sister's sake. "What is this about?" she demanded.

"It's very simple," Duane said. "You have something I want. Cooperate with me and I'll let your sister go."

Leah looked at Sarah, whose brown eyes silently pleaded for help. At twenty-two, she had just begun her first job, working at the

State Department. She was engaged to the man she had dated all through college. She was a sweet, optimistic person who had never made an enemy. And right now she looked absolutely terrified, ghost white and shaking so hard Leah could hear her teeth chatter. "All right," Leah said. "Let her go now and I'll do whatever you want."

Duane nodded and one of the other men walked to the door of the apartment and opened it. Sarah looked at the man, then at Leah. "Please let my sister come with me," she said.

"You let us worry about your sister," Duane said. "Unless you want to stay here with her."

Sarah turned to Leah again, tears in her eyes. "Go!" Leah urged. "I'll be fine."

Sarah nodded, then fled, out the door and down the street. Leah closed her eyes, remembering the relief that had flooded through her—a false hope that everything was going to be all right that Duane soon destroyed.

"What did he want?" The words burst from Travis, who had kept his promise to remain silent until now. Leah couldn't blame him for asking. She had asked herself the same question a thousand times in the past six months.

"He wanted a lot of things," she said. "Little things at first. He told me I had to break up with you, but first I had to tell him everything I knew about you." She was glad he couldn't see her face in the dark, glad he couldn't read the shame of those interrogations, when she had broken down weeping and begged Duane to believe she didn't know anything about Travis's work with the FBI. "In the end, he realized I couldn't tell him anything useful.

"He wanted me to tell him secrets about the senator, and to use my influence to find out more."

"Senator Wilson headed the Senate Committee on Homeland Security," Travis said.

"Yes. He asked me to steal paperwork from her office. I refused."

"Did he hurt you?" He gripped her wrist so hard she winced, fury vibrating through him.

She gently pulled away from him. "What he did to me physically didn't matter as much as the other ways he hurt me," she said. "He killed Sarah. He made it look like an accident, but I know he was responsible. He made sure I knew."

Travis swore, and he pulled her close, cradling her in his arms. She pressed her face into his chest and blinked back tears. "You should have called me," he said. "I would have helped."

"I thought you hated me for dumping you the way I did," she said. "And I was so afraid you'd be the next to die. Duane told me he would kill you, and I believed him. I've never met anyone as ruthless as he can be."

"So you gave him the senator's secrets," he said.

"Yes. Though nothing I told him seemed especially incriminating to me. She was an honest woman. I didn't know about any backroom deals or scandals. All I could tell him was about legislation she had proposed and issues she was interested in. But when she resigned three weeks later, I felt so guilty. I thought her resignation was my fault—that Duane had used something I had told him to drive her from office. Then I learned her husband had cancer and she wanted to spend more time with him. I don't think even Duane could give someone cancer."

"Senator Wilson resigned five months ago," he said. "What happened after that?"

"Duane took control of my life. I didn't have a job anymore. I came home one day and he had

had someone move all my belongings out of my apartment and cancel my lease. He moved me in with him. He made me sign over everything to him—my car, all my money, even the cabin here in Colorado that I'd inherited when my parents died." Saying the words now made it sound so bizarre. How could a stranger make an independent adult woman do something like that? Looking back, it was as if he had brainwashed her with terror. "I should have fought back," she said. "I should have refused his demands, but I was so afraid." She buried her face in her hands. "Why wasn't I stronger?"

Travis caressed her shoulder. "He knew how to manipulate you," he said. "You probably weren't the first person he had controlled that way."

"It doesn't even seem real now," she said. "After a while I was just…numb. Paralyzed."

"Why did he choose you?" Travis asked. "Was it only because of the senator?"

"I don't know why he chose me," she said. "Though I've thought about that a lot."

"Maybe it was just random," Travis said. "You were unlucky."

She shook her head. "Duane never acts without a reason. He's very methodical and focused. More like a machine than a man at times." A vicious, horrible machine. "Maybe at first it was because of my connection with Senator Wilson. Or maybe it was because of the other things I had. You know I inherited quite a bit of money from my parents. And he was really interested in the family cabin."

"The one on the old mining claim?" Travis asked.

"Yes. You remember when we visited there— it's in the middle of nowhere. It doesn't even have electricity or plumbing. But he asked me dozens of questions about it." When she was a child, her family had spent a month in the remote mountain cabin every summer. She and Sarah had played "prospector," gathering chunks of rocks and bouquets of wildflowers, and her parents indulged in long hikes and lazy afternoons drinking gin and tonics on the cabin's front porch and watching spectacular sunsets. She had never thought of the cabin as having value to anyone other than her family. "When Duane announced we were moving to Colorado, I was sure we were headed there," she said. "But I should have known that wasn't his style. He likes his comforts, and he has plenty of money to indulge them."

"Maybe he chose you because he wanted someone he could bully." Travis's embrace around her tightened again, more gentle this time.

"I wondered if maybe he chose me because of my ties to you," she said. "I worried about that. A lot."

"Because he thought you could give him information about investigations I was involved in?"

"More as a way of getting back at an FBI agent. He hated the Feds. He felt they had singled him out for harassment."

"He's right about that. The man is responsible for the deaths of at least a dozen people. And now that I know what he's put you through..." He kissed the top of her head, the gentlest brush of his lips that brought her close to tears again. He smoothed his hand down her back, caressing, and she stiffened.

"There's something else you should know," she said. "About me and...and Duane."

His hand stilled. Though he didn't move, she felt him pulling away emotionally. "You lived with him for months," he said. "He told people you were his wife." He swallowed hard. "Were you lovers?"

"Not willingly," she said.

"He raped you."

"Yes. Though after a while, I learned not to resist. I just…I pretended I wasn't there." She felt small and dirty when she said the words, but she fought past that. "I did what I had to do to survive," she said.

"You were strong." He caressed her back again. "I'm going to stop him. I promise. He'll pay."

"And I'm going to help." She rested her hand, palm down, over his heart, reassured by the steady rhythm of it. "I don't know if I can make you understand what a gift you gave me when you arrested me this morning."

"I was angry with you. I didn't understand."

"And I didn't expect you to. But when you took me away from that house, from Duane and his group, it was as if you broke a spell he had over me. You gave me hope—something I'd lost."

"I should have come after you before now," he said. "I should have realized that note was a lie."

"If you had come after me when I first left you, Duane would have killed you. That's why I never returned your calls or texts, and I avoided all the places we might run into each other. I didn't want to hurt you, but I was terrified of what he might do to you."

"He won't get away with this."

"He's going to keep coming after us," she said.

"Because he knows how damaging your testimony against him could be."

"Partly that, but also because he's a man who doesn't like to lose. I once saw him kill one of his team members because the man beat him at a poker game and made the mistake of laughing about it."

"He thinks you belong to him now, and he doesn't want to give you up."

The words hurt to hear, even though she knew they were true. But she didn't want Travis to believe them. "I don't mean anything to him," she said. "But he won't let the FBI get the better of him if he can help it. And he has a lot of people and resources on his side. It's frightening how many followers he's recruited to the cause."

"What is his cause?" Travis asked. "Or rather, what does he say is his cause?"

"He's convinced the United States government is irretrievably corrupt and headed down the wrong path, so it's up to people like him to correct the course. He's persuaded himself and a lot of other people that he's going to save the country by destroying everything he thinks is wrong with it."

"Including us," Travis said.

"He won't stop until he's dead." A shiver ran through her, and she clung to him even tighter. "Or we are."

Chapter Seven

Travis lay awake a long time after Leah had fallen asleep. Her description of her ordeal—and his own imagination supplying details she hadn't provided—made sleep impossible. He saw the hatred he had nursed for her for what it was now: armor around his hurt feelings. He had thought he was the strong one, carrying on despite her betrayal, yet she was the one who had suffered so much in an attempt to protect him.

He couldn't say what his feelings were for her now. Guilt and relief combined with tenderness and the desire to protect her, but all of that was mixed up with a continued wariness. Too much had happened for them to simply pick up where they had left off. When they were both safe again—tomorrow, he hoped—they both had some healing to do.

Weariness eventually overcame the turmoil in his mind and he slept, and woke to gray light and the first hint of coming dawn through the trees. Leah stirred beside him. "We should go," he said. "We have a lot of ground to cover."

They disassembled their shelter and scattered the branches, then ate a breakfast of protein bars and the last of the plums she had found the day before. She didn't bring up the conversation they had had the night before. He was relieved. Hearing about her ordeal had been difficult enough in the darkness, where he couldn't look into her eyes or see her expression. He didn't know if he was ready to face those things in the daylight.

When they had finished eating, he spread the map between them and, wearing the headlamp, studied the contour lines and landmarks noted on its surface. He had thought he could determine where they were by following the creek from the road, and guessing how far they had walked yesterday. But the crooked blue line branched into half a dozen different streams and drainages as it wound through the wilderness area.

Stumped, he refolded the map and looked around them, at the thick forest that appeared the same here as it had a mile away and a mile from that. "We'll have to climb and try to get above the tree line to figure out where we are," he said. "We're more likely to get cell service up higher, too."

"It would be good if we could find a trail," she said. "There are a lot of hiking trails in the wilderness. It's popular with hikers and back-packers."

He stowed the map in the side pocket of the pack. "Let's get some more water and head west," he said. "That should take us up into the mountains."

"What about Duane?"

"We'll keep an eye out for him. If he comes after us, we'll either run or make a stand, which-ever way seems best." He hesitated, then dug the Glock out of the other side of the pack, where he had stashed it when he put Buck's Ruger in his holster instead. "Take this." He handed her the Glock. "Do you remember how to use it?" He had made it a point to take her to the range a few times after their relationship had gotten serious, where they had run through the basics.

"Yes."

"Use it if you have to."

She nodded solemnly, then tucked the gun into the small of her back.

THE GUN FELT heavy and ominous at Leah's back, a reminder that they were still in danger. Travis hadn't said anything this morning about her ordeal with Duane, or about all she had revealed the night before. He had never been one to react emotionally to situations. His calmness had been one of the things that initially attracted her to him. Of course, sometimes his tendency to overanalyze drove her nuts, but she could usually tease him out of any broodiness.

She was in no mood for teasing now. She wanted to shake him and demand to know what he was thinking, but that would only make him clam up more. She would have to wait him out while he processed everything she had told him.

They quickly fell into a rhythm, the aches and pains of the day before fading somewhat as their muscles warmed. After a stop by the stream for more water, using the filter they had found in the pack, Travis took out the compass and studied it. He pointed toward a gap in the trees ahead. "If we head this way and stay mostly due west, we should be high enough in the mountains in a few hours that we can figure out our next move."

She hoped that included finding a cell signal that would allow them to call in the cavalry, complete with a rescue helicopter, hot food and clean clothes.

An hour passed, then two, with no sign of Duane. If not for the potential danger they were in, it might have been a pleasant day's hike. They passed through groves of golden aspen and fragrant expanses of spruce and pine, serenaded by birdsong and the chatter of squirrels. Once Travis put a hand on her arm to stop her, and pointed out a porcupine a short distance away, quills vibrating gently as it trundled away from them.

After a couple of hours they stopped to drink and rest a bit. "I'm nervous, not knowing what Duane is up to," she said.

"Do you think he spent the night in the woods?" Travis asked. "You said he liked his comforts."

"I think he would leave and gather reinforcements," she said. "He would also be concerned about the FBI getting into the house while he was away, though he probably had men guarding it and carrying away or destroying anything incriminating."

"What was he doing in Colorado?" Travis asked. "Why Denver, and why Durango now?"

Here it was, the questioning she had been waiting for. Now that he had absorbed the details of her captivity, the investigator in him wanted to know what evidence she could supply to help him in his case.

"I have no idea why we came here," she said. "Denver was for the bike race, although that was what he called a peripheral—something extra that wasn't his main goal but would enhance his reputation and make an impact. Those were all his words, not mine."

"So he was involved in the bombings at the bike races?"

"He supplied the bombs and transportation, and worked out all the logistics with Danny. But going after bike races specifically was Danny's deal. He had a grudge against racers. Duane was happy enough to go along."

"What was his main purpose, then?"

"I don't know."

Travis's skepticism was transparent, at least to her. "I don't," she insisted. "He made sure I wasn't in the room when he discussed 'business,' and he always had one of his thugs watching to make sure I didn't eavesdrop or snoop. I thought the less I knew the safer I'd be, though I realize now how foolish that was."

"But coming to Durango had something to do with his main purpose?"

"Yes, but I could never figure out what that was. He often left for a few hours or most of a day. He usually took at least one other man with him, but he never said where he was going or what he did while he was away."

"Did he do that in Denver, too? Go away?"

"Sometimes in Denver he would go away for a day or two. He always left at least one and often two men to guard me. Of course, he didn't call it that. He said the men were there to look after me. But I knew they had orders to kill me if I tried to escape."

"Did you ever try to run away?"

She felt the censure behind the words. She

had expected this, too. Travis was the type who would fight to the death for his freedom. He couldn't understand why she hadn't fought harder to leave Duane.

"He killed my sister." She couldn't keep her voice from shaking at those words. "He took everything from me—not only my possessions, but my self-confidence. I couldn't fight him. I didn't think I had anything to fight for."

"You're strong," he said. "You always have been."

"He made me weak. Haven't you ever felt that way? Helpless?"

He looked away, and despair dragged at her. Of course he hadn't. Travis had never been forced to bend to someone else's will.

"I've only felt that way once," he said, all the challenge gone from his voice. "Only when you left me."

Chapter Eight

"We'd better get going." Travis slipped the pack onto his back and started up a faint path, probably made by animals, that wound through the trees. He didn't want to see pity or disdain in Leah's eyes now that he had revealed his weakness. That's what the admission felt like—a defeat. He had let her get the better of him, and now she knew it. He had spent years learning to hide any vulnerability, yet he had let down his guard with her. Doing so felt like a big mistake. When someone knew your weakness, they could use it against you.

The shuffle of her footsteps on the forest floor assured him she was following. Despite the tough pace he had set all morning, she was keeping up. She had always been stronger than he gave her credit for. Her ordeal with Braeswood proved that. He understood she hadn't really betrayed him. She had only done what she thought was necessary to save him, even though he hadn't needed saving. He could forgive her.

He just wasn't sure he could ever forget.

"We're really starting to climb now, aren't we?"

She sounded out of breath, so he slowed and allowed her to catch up. The trees were farther apart now, allowing them to walk side by side. "If we weren't lost and running from a killer, I might enjoy this," she said. "It's so beautiful. It reminds me of backpacking trips I took with my family." Sadness clouded her eyes, and he knew she was thinking of her sister.

She might see beauty in the wild scenery, but he couldn't forget the danger. "Does Braeswood have a plane?" he asked.

"A plane?" She frowned. "I don't think so. Though he could probably hire one."

"I'm beginning to think that might be the only way he finds us." He glanced up toward the swath of blue visible between the tree tops. "Even then, he would have a hard time spotting us. He made a mistake, not tracking us all night."

"Other people make mistakes, not Duane."

He sent her a sharp look, which earned him a wan smile.

"Hey, I'm just quoting his own words," she said. "He's convinced that's the reason he'll succeed when others fail."

"That kind of arrogance will get him into trouble." Travis filed the information away. Arrogance was a weakness.

She listed to one side, wincing. "What's wrong?" he asked, taking her arm to steady her. "Are you hurt?"

"Just a stitch." She rubbed at her side. "I'll be fine."

"You need a walking stick." Once they started to climb, such an aid would come in handy for both of them. "Hang on a minute." He slid his multi-tool from the pocket of his pants and moved off the trail a little to cut two stout branches to use as walking sticks. He trimmed them smooth, then handed one to her. "You can use it as a club if you have to," he pointed out.

She hefted the stick. "I'll keep that in mind if we meet any bears."

"I'm more worried about two-legged predators."

"It was a joke, Travis. Remember those?"

"Excuse me if I don't feel like joking."

"We're going to get through this. And it helps sometimes to see the humor."

Her attitude amazed him. "You can say that, after all you've been through?"

"Life is full of bad things. Knowing that makes the good things all the more precious. I didn't always realize that on the worst days, but I see it now."

"You aren't saying this is a good day?"

"I'm not trapped with Duane." She started to say something else, then shook her head. "Anyway, we're going to get out of this. We've come too far not to." She moved past him, setting a brisk pace up the trail.

He fell in step behind her, letting her take the lead for a while. The view was definitely better from here, he thought, as he watched her hips sway provocatively as she negotiated the trail. She had always had a sunny, optimistic outlook on life. That she was able to maintain such an attitude after all she had suffered moved him. What had she been about to say just now? That she was glad to be with him again? Not that he had given her much to be glad about. He had arrested her, interrogated her and taken out his mixed-up feelings on her. She deserved better. One more reason they shouldn't be together.

They stepped from the woods into an open meadow, the charred trunks of long-dead trees marking the spot where a wildfire had cleared the area. Wildflowers formed a crazy quilt of color across the rolling landscape, painting the ground with pink and yellow and purple and white. On the other side of the meadow, the terrain rose quickly, transforming from woodland to the rocky slope of a mountain, its peak frosted with pockets of last winter's snow.

Leah stopped and leaned on her walking stick. "We ought to be able to see a long way from up there," she said.

Travis took out Buck's cell phone and checked the screen. "No signal," he said. He studied the peak again, then turned his back to Leah. "Get the map out of the pack," he said. "Maybe I can figure out where we are."

They held the map between them and studied it. Leah frowned. "None of it makes sense to me," she said. "Not without roads or landmarks or something to give me a starting point."

"One mountain isn't enough for us to go on," he agreed. He swept his hand over the closely spaced contour lines along one side of the map. "This place is full of mountains."

"So what do we do?" she asked.

He refolded the map and handed it to her. "We keep walking. If we get high enough, we should be able to figure out something."

"Let's hope the weather continues to cooperate." She peered up at a band of fluffy white clouds that drifted over the peaks. "This is the time of year when afternoon thunderstorms roll in."

"I can still walk in the rain," he said.

"It's not the rain we have to worry about." She moved around behind him to replace the map. "We don't want to be up on bare rock during a lightning storm."

"Then we'd better get moving and hope we can beat out any storms."

After a few minutes of zipping and unzipping compartments and arranging and rearranging the contents of the backpack, she handed him one of the protein bars. "We need to keep up our strength," she said.

"How many are left?" he asked.

"Just one." She glanced at the rocky peak ahead. "There isn't going to be anything we can eat up there."

"As long as we have water, we can go a long time without food." He bit into the protein bar.

It must have been in Buck's pack for a while, since it was like chewing beef jerky. Without the beef.

Leah sipped from her water bottle and regarded the protein bar skeptically. "Maybe it would help if I pretended this was something else. What's the best meal you ever ate?"

"The best?" He pondered the question. "I don't know. Probably a good steak somewhere. A big, juicy rib eye." His mouth watered and his stomach cramped at the thought. A steak would be heavenly right now, sizzling and juicy, so tender he could cut it with a fork…

"Mine is lobster," she said. "Do you remember that lobster we had at Chez Antoine? With the lemon butter, and the pesto potatoes." She closed her eyes and made a little humming sound of pleasure that made him forget all about his stomach and think of other appetites, as sharp and urgent as any need for food.

"Yeah, that was some meal," he said, barely able to get the words out. He and Leah had eaten lobster at Chez Antoine the night he proposed. He had given her the ring after the waiter served their chocolate mousse, and the manager had sent over a bottle of champagne in celebration after Leah said yes.

She still had her eyes closed, so he felt free to study her face. The past few months of hardship were written in the hollowed cheeks and faint lines around her eyes, but the maturity of the woman before him now attracted him even more than the youthful perfection he had known in their earlier time together.

A smile curved her full lips. Was she really only thinking about that succulent lobster, or was she, like him, remembering more? Was she remembering the way he had held her close in the back of the cab on the way to her apartment? Or the way they had slowly undressed each other and then made love, not merely as boyfriend and girlfriend, but as future husband and wife? That night, he felt they had already made a lasting commitment to each other.

The day he found her letter telling him she was leaving, his whole world had tilted. Suddenly, nothing in his life made sense, and for a long while, he hadn't trusted his own judgment. The revelations of the past twenty-four hours had left him just as off-kilter and uncertain.

He turned away and stashed his water bottle in the pack once more. "Come on," he said. "We've still got a long way to go."

THE TRAIL SNAKED steeply up the mountain, trees giving way to low shrubs and finally, bare rock as they climbed above the tree line. A haze obscured the landscape in the distance, so that all Leah could see was the forest they had walked out of and the rocky uplift they were climbing toward.

And Travis. She could definitely see him. His tall, broad-shouldered figure filled her vision and her thoughts. As close as they had been physically in the past twenty-four hours, he still held himself apart from her. She didn't know whether to weep with sadness over the way he was rejecting her or to shake him for being so stubborn. Was it hurt pride that made him so reluctant to rekindle the warm feelings they had once had for each other, or something worse? Did he think she was lying about Duane forcing himself on her? Or about the hold he had over her that had kept her from leaving him?

When they had stopped on the trail earlier, she had almost told him how much it meant to her to be with him again—how during her worst days, thoughts of him safe and memories of the love they had shared had kept her going. But she had held back, afraid of looking foolish or worse, seeing rejection in his eyes.

She had purposely reminded him of the dinner where they had gotten engaged. She had hoped recalling their love for each other back then would soften his attitude toward her. But again he had turned away.

Ten yards ahead of her up the trail, he stopped and pulled out the phone. "Still no signal," he said as she approached.

"No telling where the nearest cell tower is." She scanned the horizon for any sign of a tower, but saw nothing but rocky peaks and a valley of green and gold spread out beyond. Somewhere down there were other people, hikers and campers searching for solitude and adventure in the wilderness, or peak baggers hoping to check another mountain off their life list. One of those people might help them to safety. But she would be hesitant to approach a stranger, fearful of endangering them if Duane came after her and Travis. Or worse, what if the person she approached worked with Duane?

She had learned early on in her association with him that most terrorists didn't provide any visual clues. Duane's followers included housewives and doctors, military men and preachers and successful businessmen. They gave him money and followed his orders and believed he was the means to their salvation.

Travis shoved the phone back into his pocket. "If we keep moving, we're bound to eventually get a signal or reach a road or something."

She nodded, though the wearier and hungrier she became, the more her optimism faded. She didn't want to have finally escaped Duane only to die here in the wilderness.

She pushed the thought away. She hadn't come this far, held on to life this tightly, to lose it now. For a time, Duane had made her feel helpless, even hopeless. She wasn't those things anymore. She was strong. A survivor. And she would survive this ordeal, too.

The higher they climbed up the mountain, the steeper the trek. She labored to breathe in the thin air and lagged farther and farther behind Travis, so that he was forced to stop and wait for her more often. "You're doing great," he said, when she caught up with him near the top of the peak. "We're almost there."

"Almost" proved to be another hour of climbing, but at last no other rock outcroppings or false summits blocked their view. After a last scramble over loose rock and boulders, they reached their goal. Travis, who was hiking ahead of her, stopped and extended his hand to pull her up beside him onto a narrow ledge. "We did it," he said, wrapping his arms around her. "What an incredible view."

From this elevation, they could see for miles,

the world a child's play set spread out before them, with a miniature forest, rocky hills and golden valleys; sun and shadow played across them like spilled paint from a clumsy artist. The scene was both beautiful and intimidating, with no roads or houses or other people as far as the eye could see. How would they ever find their way to safety across such vastness?

"You're very quiet," Travis said. "Are you okay?"

"I'm worried about the weather." She tore her gaze from the view below to stare up at the sky. All morning, the sun had played hide-and-seek with the clouds and the temperature had dropped.

"The clouds don't look serious to me," he said. "We'll be okay."

As if to contradict him, a stiff breeze kicked up, pushing her into him. She had no room to move away, even if she could have found the willpower to do so. His warm, strong arms around her made her feel so safe and reminded her so much of when her life had been good and they had been happy together.

She forced herself not to think of that, or to contemplate the way his arms brushed the side of her breasts or the way her heart sped up as he shifted against her. She turned her eyes again to the view below. "It's like being in a plane," she said. "Everything down there looks so small and far away."

"I can see a river." He pointed, and she followed his gaze to a narrow ribbon of silver threading through the trees.

"We can see other peaks from here, too." She nodded toward the mountains that jutted up around them. "Maybe we can figure out where we are."

"Get the map." He released her and turned so that she could unzip the pack. As she pulled out the map, the wind threatened to rip it from her hand.

"Don't let it go," she said, wrinkling the plastic-coated paper as she clutched it tightly. The map was their best chance of navigating out of here.

"Turn toward the mountain," Travis said. "We'll shield the map with our bodies."

Carefully, she did as he instructed. They huddled together, the map between them, and she tried not to think about the thousand-foot drop at her back. All she had to do was stand still and not move.

Travis studied the map, forehead furrowed in concentration, then stabbed at a blue line on the paper. "That's the Animas River. I think that's what we're looking at."

"That's one of the largest rivers in this part of Colorado," she said. "Do you see anything else familiar?"

"That tallest peak to our north might be Mount Eolus." He indicated the jagged peak that rose above the others in their view. "My best guess is that we're standing on either Mount Kennedy or Aztec Mountain. If we head slightly northwest, that will take us to the Needle Creek Trail." He traced the dashed line that marked the trail on the map. "That will take us to a bridge over the river, and the Needleton Station for the Durango & Silverton Narrow Gauge Railway. We can flag down the train, and in Durango or Silverton I can call for help."

She let his words sink in, then turned to stare across the valley once more. The glinting silver thread through the trees, and the railroad that followed its banks, seemed so far away. And yet so tantalizingly close. As she stared, a thin trail of smoke rose up from the trees.

"There's the train," Travis said. His arm came around her once more and together they watched as the engine with its line of cars emerged from the trees, looking like a child's toy, puffs of white smoke marking its path.

"How long do you think it will take us to reach it?" she asked.

"It's only a couple of miles to the trail on the map, but it's rugged country. We may have to detour more than once. After that, it's only about seven miles to the train station. We probably won't make it to the trail before dark, but we can get close, and finish the trip tomorrow."

"The trains run twice a day," she said. "I remember that from some tourist brochures the leasing agent for the house left us."

"Did you ever ride it when you were a kid?" he asked.

"We rode it a couple of times, when we had relatives visiting who wanted to see the area. The scenery is spectacular, but the most fun for me and Sarah as kids was moving between the cars and hanging out the windows of the open cars to watch the engine as it puffed along the curves." She smiled, remembering the fun of exploring the train with Sarah, their parents and visiting relatives engrossed in the scenery. "I remember one time in Silverton, the town staged a mock shoot-out in the street in front of the depot. It was like traveling back in time."

"We'll get an early start and try to catch the morning train," Travis said.

"Should we try the phone again?" she asked.

He pulled out the phone once more and turned it to show her that there was still no signal. "No towers in the wilderness area," he said. "But my team will be looking for us. We could meet up with them before too much longer."

"How will they know where to look?" she asked. "We must be miles from where we started."

"That's true," he said. "But they won't give up

until they find us. In the meantime, we won't wait for them. We've got a hard hike ahead of us. Are you ready?"

"Yes." Her heart fluttered with a mix of excitement and dread. The distance they needed to cover over such rugged terrain still intimidated her, but having a goal in sight and a plan to get there made her feel stronger. Anything could happen over the next twelve hours or so, but they were going to make it, she was more sure than ever.

Another strong gust of wind threatened to knock them from their perch, and raindrops the size of BBs pelted them. "We're getting off the mountain just in time," she said, raising her voice over the drumbeat of rain on the rocks.

"Wait just a minute," Travis said, unclipping the binoculars from his belt. "I want to take a closer look, see if I can make out a trail."

She ducked her head as the rain began to fall

harder while Travis focused the binoculars to the north. "How does it look?" she asked.

"Steep. Rocky. But doable if we're careful. I'm trying to see if I can spot the trail…" His voice trailed off, then he swore, the sudden sharp exclamation rocking her back on her heels.

"What is it?" She clutched at his arm. "What's wrong?"

He lowered the glasses, his expression grim. "I found the trail," he said. "There's a big party headed up it. I'm pretty sure it's Braeswood. And it looks like he's brought in reinforcements."

Chapter Nine

Travis ignored the rain pelting his face and soaking his clothing as he studied the line of men snaking their way down the distant trail. Even with the binoculars, they resembled a line of ants. Black-clad ants carrying heavy packs and marching with military purpose up the trail.

"Are you sure it's them?" Leah asked.

"I can't be sure at this distance." Though he had memorized the faces of thousands of people, he had to be close enough to see details in order to use that talent. "But my gut tells me it's them." Casual hikers didn't move that way, or carry so much gear.

She clung to his arm. "Have they spotted us?"

"I don't think so. At least, they're not stopping to look this way." They were covering ground quickly, though. Men on a mission. Hunters out for prey.

He stashed the binoculars and made sure the pack was secure, then took Leah's arm. "Come on," he said. "We'd better get moving."

The rock was slick from the rain, and they were already soaked to the skin from the torrents of water pelting them. "Careful!" he called, reaching out to steady her as she slipped on the loose gravel.

"I'm okay," she said, pushing him away. "Just hurry. We need—"

Thunder, like a cannon shot, drowned out the rest of her words. She screamed as the rain turned to hail, ice pellets the size of grapes bombarding them. He glanced over his shoulder toward the river, no longer visible through the storm. Would the weather slow down their pursuers, or would they press on?

He and Leah had no choice but to keep moving. They had to get down off this peak, and fast. "Come on," he said, moving past her. "This way."

She remained still, rain plastering her hair to her head, glinting on her lashes like tears. "You're planning to move toward them?"

"It's our best chance to reach safety."

"We'll run right into them."

"Not if we're careful. We'll evade them and go around them. There's a lot of territory out there, and they can't cover it all."

She glanced toward the distant trail and the men who were invisible to the naked eye. "They'll know we'll head for the train station. It's the closest way out of here."

"Yes. They'll probably have someone watching. We'll have to find a way to get past."

She seemed to consider this, her expression as serious as if she were weighing the pros and cons of undergoing surgery.

"It's either go forward toward the train station or go back," he said. "It's at least three days' hiking to any kind of road. Maybe longer to safety." He didn't mention that Braeswood might very well have a second crew hiking in from that direction, intending to trap them in the middle.

Another crash of thunder shook the air, jarring her from her stupor. "All right," she said. "Let's hurry."

Descending with any speed proved challenging, with the rain and hail obscuring their vision and making the footing treacherous. The loose rock scree slid from beneath their boots, so that every step threatened to send them careering down the steep slope. Thunder shook them, and lightning exploded behind them, the light blinding and the air sharp with the smell of ozone.

"We've got to find shelter!" he shouted, and grabbed her hand.

"We're on bare rock. There is no shelter."

He'd been an idiot, ignoring her concerns about the weather. Now they were going to end up another statistic, among the half dozen or so climbers who died each year because their desire to reach a summit overruled their common sense.

"Come on." He tugged at her hand. "We have to move down."

They half ran, half slid down the next stretch of bare rock. The hail stopped, replaced by rain in silver sheets, water running in streams down the rock. Thunder crashed in percussive waves, and lightning bathed the air in eerie blue light. The hair on Travis's arms stood up and the back of his neck prickled. He gritted his teeth, bracing himself for the strike he was sure would come, but it did not.

"Look over there!" Leah stopped and pointed. He followed her gaze to a dark shadow on the side of the mountain.

"What is it?" he asked.

"I think it's a cave. Or maybe a mine tunnel."

Before she had finished speaking, he was pulling her toward it. They needed shelter, and even a hole in the ground might be enough to save them.

They had to walk sideways along a narrow ledge to reach the cave, a shallow opening beneath a rock ledge. It smelled of animals, and a faded, crushed beer can testified that they were not the first humans to use it as a refuge. He ducked inside and Leah followed. She dropped to the ground, panting and wide-eyed. "I've never been so terrified in my life," she said.

"We should be okay now." He stirred a pile of rubbish at the back of the cave with his walking stick—twigs, paper, moss and bark made a messy nest of sorts, but otherwise it was empty.

"Looks like a pack rat." Leah wrinkled her nose. "That's probably the smell, too. Let's hope the rat itself is long gone." She struggled out of the fleece jacket and wrung water from it. "I'm soaked."

"We need a fire," he said. The nest would make a good starter, but they needed bigger wood to burn if they wanted to get enough of a blaze to warm and dry them.

"I guess Braeswood's men wouldn't notice a fire way up here," she said. "Not with all the rain."

Travis raked the rat's nest to the opening of the cave, then took out his multi-tool and began sawing at his walking stick. "What are you doing?" she asked.

"We need the wood for fire. I'll need your stick, too."

She didn't protest, but handed over the stick. Within a few minutes he had a neat pile of kindling beside him. He took the matches and tinder from the pack and quickly had a blaze going.

"Too bad we don't have marshmallows," she said.

"I never liked roasted marshmallows," he said, carefully feeding one of the sticks to the flames. "Though I wouldn't say no to a nice sausage."

"Stop it. You're torturing me."

He sat back, watching the wood catch and the flames flicker bright gold. They had needed this, to stop and warm themselves by a fire, and rest in a place where they felt safe. Even if Braeswood's men did notice them up here, it would take hours of climbing for them to reach this spot, and by then he and Leah would be long gone.

"This feels so good," she said, scooting closer to him and stretching her hands toward the blaze. "I don't know what it is about a fire that's so comforting."

"It's probably genetic," he said. "Our cavemen ancestors looked to fire for protection and warmth."

"Hmmm." She let out a long sigh. "I think the rain is already letting up."

"We'll stay here until it stops and we dry off," he said. "The rest will do us good."

He fed another stick to the blaze. "Besides, we might as well use up the wood I cut."

"I'm going to miss my walking stick," she said.

"I'll cut you another one when we get down to the tree line," he said.

"Who knew you were such a woodsman?" Her smile was gentle and teasing, and he felt the familiar pull of longing for her. He forced himself to look away, focusing on the fire. She wasn't the woman he had known before, and he wasn't the same man. Whatever they had shared before, that was gone now. Trying to re-create it would be a mistake.

"You know what I've been up to for the past six months," she said. "But what have you been doing?"

Missing you. But no point going there. "Working. I was in Denver last month. I took a week this spring to go to Texas and see my folks." What could he possibly tell her that would sound interesting? His life was routine and boring, except for his work, which he couldn't talk about. "You remember my friend Luke?"

"Of course." She smiled—the same smile most women got when they thought of Luke, who was movie-star handsome and had charm to spare. "How is he doing?"

"He's engaged. To a sports reporter he met in Denver."

"Engaged! How wonderful for him. Do you like her?"

"I do." Morgan Westfield was smart and funny and she had courage to spare. "She's a lot like you, really. A strong woman."

She leaned forward to add a stick to the fire. "I'm happy for them, then."

He studied her profile, the smooth curve of her cheek, the slight jut of her chin, the curl of hair around her ear, and remembered the first time he had seen her—in the lunch line at their high school. He hadn't been able to stop looking at her and had followed her to her table and introduced himself. Later, when they were both grown and working in DC, he'd run into her at the Senate cafeteria, and that time he'd vowed not to let her get away.

Maybe some promises simply weren't meant to be kept.

"Will you go back to DC when this is over?" he asked.

She looked startled. "I don't know. I haven't thought about it much." She plucked a piece of gravel from the floor of the cave and rolled it back and forth in her fingers. "I never let myself think about the future when I was with Duane. It was too frightening. Too painful." She shook her head.

"You're smart, and you have good experience. You could find a job anywhere," he said.

"I'm sure employers will be lining up to hire a suspected terrorist." She made a face. "I'm sure I'll find something to do and somewhere to live when the time comes. I can't think that far ahead." She glanced at him. "What about you? What will you do when you're back in Durango?"

"Keep working on the case," he said. "Maybe go back to DC, or wherever the Bureau sends me." He shrugged. "The job doesn't make planning ahead easy." Though one time they had had big plans for a life together. They had been so optimistic and full of faith that everything would work out for the best. Braeswood had stolen that, too.

"I guess it's not so bad, living in the present," she said. "Isn't that what the Zen masters say you should do, focus on the now?"

"If that's what we're really doing." He leaned forward and stirred the coals with the last piece of firewood. "Sometimes I wonder if I'm not just stuck in the past." The past he'd had with her, when they had both been so happy. Knowing what they did now, could they be that happy again, or did that brand of bliss require a naïveté they would never have again?

He felt her gaze on him, and he wished he

hadn't said anything. He didn't want to answer any more questions or think any more about mistakes and regrets. He tossed aside the stick. "The rain has stopped," he said. "Are you ready to go?"

"I guess we'd better." She gazed out at the now-sunlit slope. "Maybe we'll get lucky and the rest of the trip will go smoothly.

Travis put out the fire, then led the way down, attempting to pick the best route while still headed northwest toward the river and the train tracks. They moved slowly, having to detour or backtrack twice to avoid cliffs from which there was no safe descent. At this rate, they wouldn't reach the tree line before dark. For now, the sun beat down, quickly evaporating the puddles that had collected during the storm, reflecting off the rock with a brightness that hurt the eyes.

Leah moved even more slowly than he did. He stopped often to check her progress. At one point when he looked back she was sitting and inching her way down the slope on her butt. "I'm going to get down this," she said. "I can't promise it will be pretty."

"Do you want to stop and rest?" he asked.

"No." She gave him a weary smile. "I'm afraid if I do I'll never get going again. I don't remember when I've been so tired."

He knew what she meant. Their brief respite in the cave had done little to relieve the bone weariness that had set in from miles of walking over rough terrain. Being hungry didn't help, either, but no sense bringing that up. The protein bar that served as lunch had done little to end the gnawing in his gut. He drank from his water bottle, then extended it to her. "I can get mine," she said.

"Save your energy. We'll share yours later."

"All right." Her eyes met his, heated and knowing, as if she, too, was remembering when they had shared moments far more intimate than drinking from the same water bottle.

She gulped down water, then returned the bottle to him and heaved herself upright once more. "Let's go," she said. "It's bound to be easier when we get off this mountain."

Less physically demanding, maybe, but hacking their way across dense woodland wilderness, with an unseen enemy gathering around them, wasn't his idea of easy.

They set out again. The sinking sun to their left cast long shadows across the rocks, and pikas, small rodents resembling a cross between a rabbit and a mouse, chattered at them from the granite rubble around them. He stepped down onto a rock that looked stable and it slid out from under him and he crashed to the ground, the impact sending a jolt of pain through him. He flipped onto his stomach and grappled at the ground, seeking purchase on the steep, slick rock. When he came to rest some ten feet down the slope, he was breathing hard, his hands scraped and bloody, a rip in the knee of his pants.

"Are you all right?" Leah called, half running, half sliding toward him.

"I'm okay." He sat up. "Just…be careful."

She stood a few feet above him, worry and weariness clouding her face, but not making her any less beautiful to him. "I'm beginning to get freaked out," she said. "I just want down off this mountain. I feel so…exposed up here."

"I know what you mean." He stood, trying to ignore the ache in his knees and back from the fall and the hours of climbing. All Braeswood and his men had to do was turn binoculars in the right direction and they would spot the two of them up here on this bare rock. He adjusted his pack and turned back down the trail. "Come on. We need to pick up the pace if we're going to make it into the trees by nightfall." He would feel better under cover, and they could plan their route for tomorrow.

"There are people who do this for fun," she said, starting down behind him. "They try to climb every one of Colorado's 14,000-foot-high peaks. Or every one of the 13,000-foot peaks."

"Some people enjoy the challenge, I guess," he said. "And if you did it with the right preparation and equipment, I can see how it might be enjoyable."

"Count me out," she said. "When I'm out of here I'm heading to a posh hotel with room ser—ahhhh!"

Her scream, and the sickening cascade of sliding rock and a falling body, tore through him. He whirled to see her flailing for purchase as she bounced down the side of the mountain like a rag doll.

Chapter Ten

Travis launched himself sideways toward Leah's falling body, like a tackle intercepting the ball carrier in a football game. He struck her hard, shoving her sideways and momentarily slowing her fall, but as he wrapped his arms around her and tried to dig his heels into the loose rock, they fell together, rolling and sliding at a terrifying pace. Rocks tore at them and he struggled to keep hold of her, trying to roll to shield her from the worst of the impact. She continued to flail, grabbing at the ground, her face a mask of terror, while he continually fought for purchase with his heels.

In the end, it wasn't their own efforts that saved them, but the bent trunk of a stunted tree that clung stubbornly to a ledge that jutted out over nothing. They came to rest against the trunk, Travis's left foot dangling in empty air. The rough bark of the tree dug into his back, but it was the most welcome pain he had known.

Leah stared at him, her eyes almost black from her fear-enlarged pupils, her skin the color of the snow that lingered in pockets on the peak. "We stopped," she whispered.

"Yeah." He buried his face against her shoulder and struggled to rein in the tidal wave of emotion that threatened to unman him. Fear that they had almost died, exhilaration that they had survived, rage that they should be in this situation in the first place and a paralyzing terror that he had almost lost her. He could talk about justice and his job and his duty to his country, but in those seconds when his life had been in the balance, the one truth he knew was that everything he had done from the moment he had laid eyes on her at Braeswood's mansion had been for her. She was the reason he was fighting so hard, the reason he was willing to risk everything.

She nudged him. "You okay?"

"Yeah." He raised his head, then sat up, slowly, keeping his back against the tree. The ledge they had come to rest on was fairly wide and level, safe enough for some of the tension to ease out of him.

She struggled into a sitting position and swept her hair out of her eyes, then glared at him. "What did you think you were doing, tackling me that way? You could have been killed."

"I had to save you."

She wiped away a smear of blood and mud on her cheek. "No, you didn't. You'd be better off without me. You could move faster on your own."

"No, I wouldn't be better off without you." He shifted to kneel in front of her and grabbed both her arms. "I never was."

He told himself he deserved the wary look she gave him. He had certainly given her plenty of reasons to not believe him, to be afraid of him even. He smoothed his hands down her arms, then gently pulled her to him. "I need you, Leah," he whispered. "I always have."

The touch of her lips and the feel of her arms tightening around him filled him with heat and light, like a powerful drug flowing through his veins. The kiss was both remembered and brand-new, the urgent pressure of her mouth against his own, the tangling of tongues and press of bodies something he had longed for and something he waited to discover.

She fell back, pulling him with her. He straddled her, one knee planted on either side of her hips, her breasts pressed against his chest, her heart like a drumbeat in counterpoint to his own. One hand tangled in his hair while the other wrapped across his back. He kissed her cheek and tasted the metallic tang of the blood drying there, and pulled back. "You're hurt," he said.

"So are you." She smoothed her hand across the dark bruise forming on his forearm where he had slammed into the rock. "But we'll be okay. We're together and we'll be okay." Then her lips found his again, silencing words and obliterating thought. Fear and doubt, aches and pains, didn't matter in the face of their need for each other. He slid his hand beneath her shirt, cupping and caressing her breast, and he pressed his growing arousal at the juncture of her thighs. She arched against him and reached for the pull of his zipper.

Something—the call of a crow or the bite of the wind at his back, or the sharp jab of a rock against his hand when he moved—pulled him out of the drugging fog of lust and need. He wrapped his fingers around her wrist. "I think maybe this isn't exactly the right time for this," he said.

She blinked up at him, then a blush warmed her cheeks. "I guess I got a little carried away," she said.

"Hey, I wasn't complaining." He sat back and helped her to sit also.

"I guess we'd better get going," she said.

"Wait." He pulled her back down and reached around for the pack. "I want to tend to that gash on your face while there's still good light."

He found the first aid kit buried in the pack and cleaned and dressed the cut on her cheek and another on her arm with antibiotic ointment and adhesive bandages. She did the same for a gash on his knee and the cuts and scrapes on his hands. The sun had dipped behind the mountains to the west, taking with it most of its light and warmth. She shivered as the wind gusted across their rocky perch, and he fought the urge to pull her close once more. He was cold, too, now that the rush of adrenaline and passion had faded.

"Come on." He stood and reached to pull her up beside him. "We've got to hurry down and find some place to spend the night."

"Right. The last thing I want is a fall like that in the dark."

Carefully, they made their way down the next steep stretch. Thankfully, the grade became more gradual after that. Soon, they reached the shelter of the trees and a deeper darkness in which the black of trees was barely distinguishable from the black of the air around them. He stopped so that they could catch their breath and to try to orient himself. "I'd rather not turn on the light," he said. "In case someone sees it."

She gripped his arm, fingers digging in. "No. Don't turn on the light. I'm more afraid of Duane and his troops than I am the dark."

"I'll cut us another couple of walking sticks," he said. "That will help us feel our way and keep our balance."

Even that simple chore took longer in the dark, and he was forced to turn on the light briefly in order to find branches of the right size and shape. He trimmed them quickly and handed one to Leah. "Thanks," she said. "At least now I have a crutch if I sprain my ankle tripping over a rock."

"Don't even think that." He tested his own stick, a stout, knotted length of cedar that would double as a cudgel. "Come on." He wanted to get deep enough into the woods to have good cover when they stopped for the night, but movement was more difficult than he had anticipated. Though the ground was more stable underfoot here, they had to constantly be on guard for tree roots, stumps and other obstacles. When he had banged his shins for the fourth time and she had tripped for the third, he took hold of her hand and pulled her to his side. "We've got to stop," he said. "Before one of us is seriously hurt."

"It's so much darker here than in the city," she said. "Darker than I ever knew it could be."

"I'm going to risk the headlamp again," he said, pulling the light out of the side pocket of the pack and slipping it on. "Just until we find a safe place to bed down."

The light cast a weak golden beam across the forest floor, enough to reveal they were in an area of closely growing trees and dense underbrush. "No wonder we kept running into things," Leah said.

"It's good cover to hide us tonight," he said,

directing the light around them. "No one's going to be able to get close without us hearing them."

"I hope you're right."

As they had the previous night, they made a shelter of tree branches in the hollow left by a fallen tree. He spread the space blanket and crawled in, then pulled her in after him and covered them both.

She snuggled against his shoulder with a weary sigh. "I'd trade a year of my life for a cheeseburger right now," she said.

His stomach growled in response. "Try not to think about it," he said.

"It's all I can think about." She turned to face him. Though he couldn't make out her features in the darkness, he sensed her face very close to him. "Distract me," she said, her breath warm against his cheek.

As tired as he was, that plea was all the invitation he needed. He slid his hand beneath her shirt and over her breast. "Does this distract you?"

"It's a start." She squirmed against him and moved her hand around to squeeze his backside. "How about you? Are you feeling distracted?"

He nuzzled her neck, sliding his tongue into the hollow of her throat, savoring the silky feel and taste of her, a mix of salty and sweet. "Distracted from what?" He pressed into her, letting her feel his arousal, then covered her lips with his own.

She opened her mouth at his invitation and tangled her tongue with his, even as she explored his body with both hands. She pushed up his shirt and trailed her fingers across his chest, leaving sensations like the bite of sparks on his flesh.

"I've missed you so much," he said, resting his forehead against hers and fighting to rein in the desire that drove him to take her now, this very minute.

"I've missed you, too." She pushed his shirt up farther and kissed his shoulder, then slid her teeth across his flesh. "I've missed making love to you." She unfastened the top button on his pants.

He stilled, his fingers tightening on her shoulders. "I'm not sure now is the right time," he said.

"Are you worried Duane and his men will find us?"

"I don't think they'll find us tonight. We're too well hidden, and he's already shown he doesn't like to search at night. He probably figures we aren't going anywhere."

"Then why?"

He shifted, trying to get comfortable—impossible, given his current state. He traced the curve of her cheek with one finger, her skin like satin. "Think about it. We're exhausted. Hungry. Filthy, lying on the ground. You deserve better than that."

"I don't care about any of that." She cupped her hand to his face. "Look at me."

"I can't see you."

Her lips curved in a smile beneath his finger. "Then feel." She grabbed his hand and laid it over her heart. "You risked your life today to save me. But it wasn't the first time you saved me. Through the worst of the times with Duane, I got through it by thinking of you. I remembered what it was like to be with you, whether we were walking in the park or making love in your apartment. I remembered how much we had loved each other, and that reminded me that I was worthy of love. A good man had cherished me once. No matter what happened to me, I had had that."

"You deserve better than the way I treated

you," he said, and kissed the corner of her eye, tasting the salt of her tears, his own eyes stinging.

"We can't change the past," she said. "And tomorrow we could die. I hope not, but it could happen. If it does, I want to spend my last night with you. All these other things—the hard ground, my empty stomach, my fear—you can make them go away for a little while."

"I want to make love to you." He wished he could see her face right now, could read the emotion in her eyes. He settled for kissing the corner of her mouth. "But I'm worried about hurting you." She had been through so much—he couldn't think of it without feeling sick.

"You can't hurt me." She slid her hands down his chest and lowered the zipper on his pants. "I trust you, Travis, and I want to be with you. And that's all that really matters right now."

LEAH HELD HER BREATH, waiting for Travis's answer. Would his lingering doubts keep him from bridging this final gap between them? Was she crazy for even wanting this, considering their situation? "I want you," he said, and kissed her, a tender, dizzying kiss that quickly turned more passionate.

Undressing in such close quarters, in pitch blackness, proved a challenge, but one they were equal to. She giggled as he helped her squirm out of her jeans and underwear, and laughed at his attempts to shed his own pants while kneeling over her. Then he leaned away, reaching behind him.

"What are you doing?" she asked.

"I had to get the condom from Buck's pack," he said.

She laughed. "Thank goodness for Buck."

"That pack has saved us more than once the past couple of days," he said.

"Yes, but you have to admit—a condom is not something most people would consider essential wilderness survival gear."

"I think I read somewhere that a condom can be used as an emergency water carrier, or as a waterproof wrap for a wounded hand or foot," he said. "That's probably the reason it was in the pack."

"Sure that was the reason." She took the packet from him and tore it open. "But we're going to put it to better use, I think." She reached for him.

Breath hissed through his compressed lips as she fit the condom to him. She smiled, enjoying this moment of control and suspense, the trembling anticipation of the joy yet to come.

Travis took her by the shoulders and urged her to lie down. He slid alongside her and pulled her to him. The sensation of his warm skin against her, the contours of his body so familiar and welcome, brought a lump to her throat.

He nuzzled her neck and kissed his way across her shoulder, his hands skimming over her torso, like a blind man rereading a familiar text he had enjoyed many times. She arched against him, urging him on.

His mouth closed over her breast and she lay back, eyes shut tight, losing herself in their lovemaking. He still remembered how to touch her, what she liked and what excited her most. And she hadn't forgotten how to make his body respond to her touch—where he liked to be stroked, how he wanted to be held.

They each moved slowly, deliberately, murmuring words of encouragement and endearment, their entire focus on pleasuring and being pleasured. And when he knelt between her legs, poised over her, she was trembling with need for him. She reached up and pulled him to her, welcoming him as if the months apart had never happened, all the hurt and shame burned away in the heat of their passion.

Her fulfillment shuddered through her in a slow wave that left her gasping and grinning like a kid at Christmas.

"You liked that, did you?" he asked, another thrust like an exclamation point at the end of a sentence.

"Y-yes," she said, her voice unsteady.

"I liked it, too." He thrust again. "A lot."

She squeezed her thighs around him and lifted her hips to meet his next advance. They fell into a familiar, urgent rhythm, her need for him spiraling upward once more, her breath coming in gasps. Somehow she had forgotten, or refused to let herself remember, how good they were together. How right.

He came with a cry and reached down to stroke her, bringing her to a quick, second climax soon after. She was still shuddering when he withdrew, discarded the condom and lay down beside her, his head on her shoulder. She trailed her fingers across his shoulders and back, tracing patterns across his smooth, warm skin. "I love you so much," she murmured.

But her only answer came in a soft snore from her exhausted lover.

Chapter Eleven

Travis woke while it was still dark, the familiar yet unexpected weight of Leah against him disorienting him, as if their months apart had been nothing more than an unpleasant nightmare. Yet the hard ground beneath him and the chill around them reminded him of their circumstances, and the dangerous gauntlet they had yet to run before they could truly heal the wounds they had both suffered.

"What time is it?" she asked, her voice holding no trace of sleepiness, though he would have sworn she wasn't yet awake.

"I don't know. Early, I think."

"I slept well, considering." She stretched, and he could imagine her smile, the one that had so often greeted him in the morning after those nights she had spent at his place.

"Me, too." Yet as slumber receded and alertness returned, the aches and pains of the previous days' treks burned at his knees and hips and back. His stomach felt hollow, too. "We should set out as soon as it's light enough to see," he said.

He found the flashlight and switched it on. The thin beam lit their tiny shelter like a candle flame. She sat up beside him, hunched against the tree branches that formed their roof, and efficiently plaited her hair and secured the end with an elastic band. She was naked still, her breasts luminous in the light, and he felt a fresh surge of desire for her. They were both hungry, dirty, bloodied and bandaged. Yet she was still the most beautiful woman he had ever known. He sat also and cupped one breast in his hand. "How are you feeling this morning?" he asked.

"Hungry, thirsty and horny—not necessarily in that order." She grinned at him. "If someone had told me I'd be sitting in a lean-to in the woods after a night of sleeping on the ground, not having had a shower or a decent meal in a couple of days, with a gang of sociopathic terrorists pursuing us, and the chief thought on my mind was how soon I could get you back in the sack, I'd have told them they were certifiable. Does that make me some kind of pervert? Or just really desperate?"

"I think desperate circumstances force us to focus on elemental needs. The fundamental drives of our animal nature." He bent to kiss the valley between her breasts. "Or maybe I'm the same kind of pervert."

She combed her fingers through his hair, then suddenly grew still.

"What is it?" he asked, sensing a change in her mood. "What's wrong?"

"Nothing. I…" She bit her lip and shook her head. "No, I don't have the right."

"The right to what?" He took her hand and brought it to his lips. "Tell me what's upsetting you."

She looked up at him through the veil of her lashes. "After I left you—were there other women? I don't blame you if there were. You're a good-looking man and you weren't attached. I just…I just wondered." Her voice trailed away and she stared at the ground between them, the picture of misery.

He traced his finger along her jaw, her skin soft as satin. "There wasn't anyone else," he said. "Not in my bed. I couldn't. Or at least, I didn't want to." He had been so angry, then hurt, then afraid of having to suffer those feelings all over again if he got too close to anyone else.

"I'm sorry I hurt you," she said. "I made what I thought was the right choice, but so much has happened that I couldn't have foreseen."

He wished she hadn't made those choices, too, but he thought he was doing a good job of handling those emotions. He kissed her forehead. "You were right last night when you said we couldn't change the past."

"What about our future? I know I said I didn't want to think about what I was going to do now that I'm free again, but ever since we talked about it up there on the mountain, it's all I *can* think about. What are we going to do when we get out of here? I'm a wanted felon and you're an FBI special agent."

"So you knew we were looking for you?" he asked.

Her expression clouded. "Duane showed me

on the computer—that I had made the FBI's Ten Most Wanted list. He seemed so pleased by the news, while I was horrified. Of course, that was the point—now that I was a wanted criminal, I had one more reason to stay with him. He convinced me that as soon as I left his protection I'd end up in prison, or even sentenced to death for acts of terrorism." She rubbed her shoulders, as if trying to warm herself against a sudden chill. "All I could think was I was glad my poor parents didn't have to suffer through that—one daughter dead and the other a criminal. And you." She raised her eyes to meet his, their normally bright brown dull and bleak. "I wondered what you thought of me. Your whole life was about upholding the law. This seemed like the final betrayal."

It had felt that way to him, too. The day the bulletin was issued adding her to the list, he'd locked himself in his office and pretended to be engrossed in computer research. But all he'd done for hours was stare at the photo of Leah on the screen. It was the picture taken for her Senate identification badge, with her facing the camera, her hair tucked behind her ears, lips curved in a coy smile, as if she might burst into laughter the moment after the camera clicked.

"Isn't that the woman you were engaged to?" Luke had asked him when they left work that afternoon. It wasn't a question he even had to ask. Like Travis, Luke was a super recognizer who never forgot a face. He'd been with Leah dozens of times over the past month and would never confuse her picture with anyone else.

But Travis knew why his friend asked. This was his chance to either discuss the situation with someone who would listen and keep his confidences, or close off the subject forever. He looked Luke in the eye and chose the latter option—the only one he could live with at the time. "It's not Leah," he said. "It's just someone who looks like her."

Luke studied him a long moment, then nodded. "Okay. That's what I'll tell anyone if they ask."

"Are you going to have to arrest me when we leave here?" Leah asked. She attempted a smile, but failed. "But I guess you already have. Isn't that what you said when you first dragged me out of the car? That I was under arrest?"

"I'm not going to arrest you," he said.

"I won't blame you if you do," she said. "You're doing your job."

"I was doing my job then. Now I know better. You were a hostage. The government won't pursue the charges against you once they know that."

"I wish I believed that. Even if the government does drop the charges against me, there will al-

ways be people who see me as part of Braeswood's group. A terrorist. Associating with me
won't be good for your career."

As much as he wanted to deny this was true,
he couldn't. Dating a woman who was currently
on terrorist watch lists across the country, not
to mention the Bureau's own Ten Most Wanted
list, could bring his career to a screeching halt,
or even mean the end of a job he loved. He
levered himself over her and stared down into
her beautiful, troubled face. She wasn't a terrorist. He was as sure of that as he was sure
of his own name. And he was sure there was
no point in wasting time worrying about what
being with her might mean to his job. Not when
they still had so much to get through to reach
safety. "Right now, all I care about is making it
safely through today," he said. "And spending
the hour or so before it's light enough to start
walking doing something a lot more pleasant

than worrying." He lowered his body, making sure she felt his arousal.

Her breath caught and her eyes glazed. "Um, that sounds good," she said, and wrapped her arms around him and pulled him close.

He kissed her, a long, leisurely enjoyment of her sensitive mouth. His hands roamed her body, delighting in the feel of her. He skimmed along her ribs and traced the line of her hip. Then his hand stilled and he let out a groan.

"What is it?" she asked, her voice full of alarm. "What's wrong?"

"We don't have another condom."

She let out a shaky breath. "It's okay. I'm still on birth control. It's a hormone implant, so I don't have to worry about missing pills or anything."

"That's great." He smoothed his hand down her shoulder, and tried and failed to keep the discomfort in his voice. "I haven't been with anyone since you left," he said. "So I know I'm healthy. But you…"

She had been with Duane. He didn't want to think about that, but there was no getting around the specter of the villain that in some ways was always between them. But he let her fill in the rest of his objection. He couldn't say the words out loud.

She bit her lip and turned her head away from him, a deep blush staining her cheeks. "He always wore a condom," she said softly. "He was very fastidious about that kind of thing. But I understand if you'd rather not…"

The pain in her voice and the realization that he was making her remember that horror cut him to the quick. He gathered her close. "I want you," he said. He brushed his lips across hers, then drew her into his arms. "I've never stopped wanting you."

She dragged her gaze back to his, some of the

light returning to her eyes. "There's no one here but us right now," she said, as much to herself as to him. "Only you and me, with nothing and no one between us."

He had made love to Leah many times, in apartments and hotel rooms and once, in a moment of daring, in a deserted conference room in the Senate building where she had worked. They had known the hesitant excitement of new partners and the frantic urgency of more experienced lovers. But none of those encounters had the intensity of these stolen moments in the pitch blackness of this crude shelter in the woods, when they relearned each other's bodies by touch and taste, aching to fulfill a need that surpassed the fear and hunger and fatigue that was like a black cloud hovering around them. Making love to Leah kept that cloud from engulfing him, at least for a little while.

They lay together for a little while afterward,

dozing, until a dusky light began to breach
the shelter, filtering down through gaps in the
overlain pine boughs. They couldn't put off the
tough day ahead any longer. He sat up. "I think
it's time to go," he said.

Another woman—another person, he cor-
rected—might have protested, begging for a
few more minutes' rest, or complaining of the
predawn chill that stung them as soon as they
pushed back the space blanket they had been
wrapped in and emerged from the lean-to. But
Leah only folded the blanket, put on her shoes,
then rummaged in the pack until she found their
last protein bar. "Breakfast," she announced,
holding it up as if she had unearthed a gold
nugget.

"You eat it," he said, even as his stomach
clenched painfully.

"Don't be so noble." She broke the bar in half
and handed him one portion. "If it comes right

down to it, I ought to give the whole thing to you. If I grow too weak to walk, you can carry me. If you faint from hunger, I couldn't do a thing about it."

"Who says I'd carry you?" he asked around a dry chunk of the stale bar.

"You would. You're wired to be a hero."

He grunted and reached for the pack. "I might surprise you."

"All right, then." She stood and looked him up and down. "Maybe you'd just do it for the sex."

TRAVIS DUG THE compass out of the pack and spent a little time orienting them toward the north. Leah looked over his shoulder. "I think they taught us how to use one of those at Girl Scout camp one year," she said. "They took us out in the woods and we had to find our way to a meeting point using a compass and a map."

"Then maybe I should give this to you," he said.

"No way." She held up her hands as if to ward him off. "I never did find the meeting point during that Girl Scout camp. I seem to recall they had to send out a search party."

He laughed and consulted the needle again. "I think I've got this figured out. At least I hope so." He hefted his stick. "North, ho!"

He led the way, pushing through the dense greenery and ducking under the low-growing branches of spruce and fir that crowded this part of the forest. He held the compass in one hand and his hiking stick in the other, using the stick to push aside tangles of vines or branches that blocked their way.

Leah struggled along behind him. She hoped the compass worked and that he was reading it correctly. Everything about this thick, shadowed woodland disoriented her. Travis had shown her on the map how, if they traveled north, they would eventually intersect the Needle Creek Trail, a well-traveled path that led from the Needleton train station to the popular Chicago Basin backcountry area. "All we have to do is keep walking north," he said.

Right. So easy. She winced as yet another thorn-covered vine whipped back to strike her in the legs, the thorns biting through her jeans. She carefully picked the vine away from her, then hurried to catch up with Travis, who was stomping through the undergrowth with all the finesse of an elephant. "If anyone is following us, they won't have any problem figuring out which way we went," she said.

"Braeswood and his men are most likely between us and the trail." He slashed at another vine with his walking stick.

She shivered. "How many men were in that

group you saw yesterday?" She should have
asked for the binoculars so she could see the hikers for herself. Even at that distance she might
have recognized Braeswood or one of his inner
circle of thugs.

"I counted eight." He held aside a leaning sap-
ling and motioned for her to move past him.
"They were fully kitted out with high-tech
gear, too. Like a SEAL team on a mission." He
shook his head. "Why is he going to so much
trouble—spending so much time and trouble—
trying to find you?"

Did she imagine the annoyance in his voice?
She didn't have to be a therapist to figure out
what had prompted the question. For a while
last night and again this morning, they had both
managed to put aside thoughts of Duane Braeswood and her complicated relationship with
the terrorist. But he always lurked in the shad-

ows, a phantasm poisoning everything good between them.

As strong and confident as Travis was in every other aspect of his life, in these past few days she had discovered how deeply she'd wounded him. Doubts about her loyalty—and maybe about his own feelings as well—worried at him. He asked the same questions of her over and over out of the very human desire for a better answer, one that would explain the unexplainable. Had she really been Duane Braeswood's unwilling mistress? Had she done anything to attract him to her? The things that had happened to her in the last six months had to have changed her, but had they changed her into a woman he could never really love? A woman who could never love him?

She struggled to find the words that would assuage his fears and bolster her own confidence. "I don't pretend to understand why Duane does anything he does," she said. "There was never any emotional connection between us. People don't mean anything to him. He used me the way he might use an inanimate object. I served some purpose in his twisted worldview, so he kept me around. I was someone he could manipulate and control. Someone he could hurt, and I think he got a kind of pleasure from that."

Travis stopped so abruptly she almost collided with him. He whirled to face her, his face a mask of pain. "He had better hope I'm never in a room alone with him," he said. "When I think of what he did to you…"

She grabbed his arm, her fingers digging into his rock-hard biceps. "Don't do this to yourself," she said. "Don't dwell on it. It's in the past now. All we can do is focus on getting out of here and doing everything we can to see that he is captured and punished."

He inhaled raggedly and nodded, regaining

his composure. She released her hold on him and took a step back, still watching him carefully. "I'm okay," he said. "And we are going to find him and see that he's punished. Your testimony will go a long way toward making that happen."

"I hope so," she said. "I don't know a lot about his operation, but I know some things, and I know the people he associated with. I don't have your memory for faces, but I think I would recognize a lot of them again."

"You probably know more than you think you do," he said. "Enough to put him away for a long time."

He checked the compass, and they set out walking again. "Don't forget that I'm not the only one Duane is after," she said. "He doesn't have any love for the Feds. You ran him down in his home, you took me away and you killed one of his men. Any one of those things could be reason enough for him to have a grudge against you."

"How many people does he have working with him? Were there more than your driver and Eddie Roland, Buck and Sam?"

"There are probably hundreds of people connected to Duane in one way or another," she said. "Some merely send money to support his efforts. Others provide information or access to a location, while others do the actual work of carrying out attacks, building bombs, intercepting intelligence and disseminating propaganda. In many ways, he operates like any head of a large international corporation."

"And Braeswood heads it all?"

"In the United States," she said. "Though I sometimes had the sense that there were other people, in other countries, who wielded power also, to the point where Duane had to answer to them." She shook her head. "But I don't have any proof of any kind of connection like that. In any case, there were always new people filtering in and out of the house. Mostly men, but a few women, too."

"Do you think you could identify them again?"

"Some of them. But I'm sure there were others I never saw. He was always on the phone, talking in a cryptic kind of code about targets and objectives and tasks. He never said anything in my presence that told me what he was really up to."

"How long would you have stayed with him if I hadn't come along?"

She couldn't see his face when he asked this question, but the stiffness of his shoulders and the chill in his voice warned her to tread carefully. "I don't know," she said. "Maybe I would have found the courage on my own to leave. Or maybe he would have grown tired of me and had me killed. There were days I would have welcomed that."

He turned and sent her a sharp look. "What happened to all that optimism and hope you were preaching about earlier?"

"I wasn't preaching. And it's much easier to be hopeful now that I'm away from that prison. I had plenty of bad days. Some truly horrible days." She closed her eyes, struggling for composure. She would never forget the things Duane had done to her, but she didn't want to let them define her.

His hand around her wrist made her open her eyes. He studied her, his expression intense, as if he were searching for something familiar in a stranger's face. "I never realized before how strong you are. I wonder what else about you I overlooked."

Then he released her and turned away to study the compass, then adjust their course toward the path that, she hoped, would take them to safety.

THE JOURNEY BECAME a forced march as they concentrated on putting one foot in front of the other, finding the best route, stopping only to check the compass and once to filter water to fill the water bottles from a small stream. Leah moved steadily behind Travis, never complaining, stopping only when he did. He had loved her and wanted to spend the rest of his life with her, but he had always thought of her as gentle and delicate. He was the strong one in their relationship—the man who was supposed to protect her. Maybe that was a sexist thing to believe in the twenty-first century, but it was a belief reinforced by both his upbringing and his training. He was an officer of the law, sworn to serve and protect.

She was smart, and funny, and incredibly sexy. But he had never known she was so tough and determined. Seeing her this way both awed and unsettled him. What other aspects of her character had he misjudged or failed to see in her? If he had been more in tune with what was going on inside her, would he have picked up on her distress over her sister? Could he have done something to help her? Could he have saved her from the hell she had suffered as the prisoner and pawn of Duane Braeswood? The idea that he had failed her weighed heavy; he wouldn't fail her again.

He stopped to check the compass again; fallen trees, dense underbrush and rocky outcroppings forced them to continually detour off a direct route. Leah moved up beside him, her hand on his arm. She rose on tiptoe and whispered in his ear. "I think I heard voices."

He looked at her sharply. "Where?"

"I can't tell which direction they were coming from. Listen."

He raised his head, straining his ears to pick out any sound beyond the sigh of wind in the branches overhead and the occasional birdsong. Her hand tightened on his biceps and he recognized the low murmur that might be distant conversation.

He pointed ahead and to their left, and indicated they should move in that direction. She pulled him back and spoke again, her mouth against his ear, the words barely audible. "What if it's Duane's men?"

"We won't know until we check it out," he said. The average backpacker wouldn't be able to save them, but they might have food or information about Braeswood's whereabouts.

"Do you still have the Glock?" he asked.

She reached behind her and withdrew the gun from the waistband of her jeans.

"Hide behind a tree here and I'll go check this out," he said. "If anyone comes after you, shoot them."

"No." She shook her head. "We'll check it out

together. It doesn't make sense for us to separate. If they do discover us, we're better off facing them as a team."

The stubborn set of her chin and the determined look in her eyes told him argument
would be a waste of time. "All right." He drew
the Ruger and checked that a round was in the
chamber. "We'll go together."

They moved slowly, carefully placing each
step and pausing often to listen to the intermit-
tent bursts of what he was sure was conversation. Whoever these men were—and the low
register of the words indicated they were men—
they weren't trained in stealth operations. They
weren't making any great effort to conceal their
whereabouts.

At last they reached a bluff overlooking the
river. A well-worn trail meandered along the
bank of the waterway, and beside this path two
men sat on a fallen tree trunk, eating lunch.

Travis was sure these were two of the men he had seen hiking in yesterday. They were dressed in black tactical fatigues, with heavy black packs resting at their sides. He could make out a holstered pistol at one man's hip—possibly another Ruger—and the blued stock of an assault rifle showed in the shadows beside the other man's pack.

"The man on the right works for Duane." Leah spoke softly in his ear. "I don't know his name, but I've definitely seen him before."

Travis nodded and started to move forward. Leah tugged on him, her expression one of alarm.

He indicated they should retreat into the woods again. When he judged they were far enough from the river that the men there wouldn't hear their whispered conversation, he stopped. "We should move around them and cross the river downstream while they're eating," she said.

"Do that and we might walk right into a trap. If they have men guarding the bridge, I'd like to know before we get there. If I can get close enough to hear their conversation I might find out more about who is here and where."

"It's too dangerous."

"The more information we have, the less danger we're in." The primary focus of his job with the Bureau was gathering information. The right knowledge often made the difference when it came to stopping criminals like Braeswood.

She worried her lower lip between her teeth, then nodded. "All right. But we'll go together."

He could have argued that two people were taking a bigger risk than one, that two people made more noise and were more likely to be seen. But he didn't want to be separated from her any more than she wanted to wait behind for him. The memory of Braeswood holding a knife to her throat when he'd left her before still sent a chill through him. "We'll go together," he agreed.

They returned to their previous position on the bluff. The two men had made another tactical mistake, stopping so near the river. The noise from the water rushing over rocks would mask sounds around them. And they were still chatting as they ate, only occasionally scanning the area. As long as he and Leah were careful, they shouldn't have too much trouble getting close enough to hear their conversation.

He touched her shoulder and indicated she should follow him through a thick growth of bushes that filled a drainage leading to the river. This cover would take them almost to the water's edge, downstream and behind the two men. From there, he hoped they would be able to listen in on their discussion. He only hoped the two were talking about their job here in the wilderness, and not their favorite sports team or women.

They crawled through the bushes on their hands and knees, a torturous progress, battling thorns and rocks and snagging branches. Fortunately, a thick layer of leaf litter covered the ground, muffling the sounds of their progress. As long as the two men didn't decide to look behind them and notice the bushes moving, he and Leah should be okay.

Very near the water, he stopped. Though the noise from the river swallowed up some of the two men's words, he could make out enough to get the gist of their conversation. It was, as he hoped, about their duties out here.

"It's a big waste of time." The older of the two, the one Leah had recognized, was a wiry, tanned fellow with closely cropped salt-and-pepper hair. He bit into an apple and chewed as he spoke. "If they aren't dead by now, they will be soon."

"Then we'd better find their bodies," the second man, a younger, beefy blond, said. "The chief isn't going to let up until he knows they're out of the picture."

"I'm going to really enjoy shooting a Fed." The older man mimed firing a pistol.

"The chief wants the woman alive," the blond said. "I think she's the real reason he's going to all this trouble."

"Women can make a man do crazy things, that's for sure." The older man finished off his apple and tossed the core into the grass at their feet. "Though I never knew what to make of the two of them together. He never paid that much attention to her. And she never looked all that happy to be there."

"Oh, I think she was happy enough. The chief is loaded, and some women really get off on the power. She was one of those types. Why else would she stick around? It wasn't like he kept her chained to the bed."

"Now there's an idea," the older man said. "I had a girlfriend once who was into that stuff. You know, bondage and whips and stuff. Pretty hot."

"Maybe when we find Braeswood's woman, we don't turn her over to him right away," the blond said. "Maybe we have a little fun with her first."

Behind Travis, Leah made a choking sound, then stumbled back.

"What was that?" The blond sat up straight and reached for the rifle.

"Something over there, in the bushes." The older man was on his feet, his gun drawn. Travis turned to look at Leah, who huddled in the underbrush, eyes as wide as a frightened rabbit's.

He started to move back toward her when the loud crack of gunfire froze him, and a bullet smacked into the dirt inches away from him.

Chapter Twelve

Leah bit down hard on her hand to keep from screaming as bullets slammed into the dirt around them. Travis surged forward and, grabbing her hand, dragged her after him. They didn't bother with stealth this time, crashing through the tangle of vines and shrubs, fighting their way up the slope. The rapid tattoo of gunfire propelled her forward with strength she hadn't known she possessed.

At the top of the bluff, Travis dived behind a large boulder and she followed him, landing with her cheek pressed to the dirt, the frantic pounding of her pulse and ragged breathing drowning out all other noise. Then a deafening blast of gunfire made her jump. She raised her head to see Travis firing down the slope. Braeswood's men returned fire and a bullet nicked the rock beside them, sending shards of granite flying, then all was silent.

"They're too well hidden for me to get a good shot," Travis said.

"At least they stopped shooting at us," she said. She had drawn the Glock and held it pointed at the ground, knowing better than to fire without a clear target.

"They're probably radioing for help," Travis muttered. "It's what I would do in their position."

"They'll try to surround us." The thought made her chest feel hollow.

"Which means we have to get out of here now." He unshouldered the pack, took out the box of ammunition and began reloading the Ruger. "We're going to run hard that way." He nodded to the west. "We're headed for the bridge. The train hasn't stopped there yet—we would have heard the whistle."

"Duane will have someone guarding the bridge," she said.

"Then we'll have to find a way past them." He shoved the gun into the waistband of his pants. "Are you ready?"

She took a deep breath. The first rush of adrenaline had faded, leaving her shaky, but she had to find a way to get past that. She wouldn't sit here and let them take her back to Duane without a fight. "I'm ready."

As soon as they began moving, the gunfire followed them, closer this time, as if their two pursuers were climbing the ridge. They retreated farther away from the bluff, into the cover of thicker underbrush, but continuing to run parallel to the river. She hoped their head start on level ground gave them an advantage.

The going was tough, and fear made it even more difficult to breathe. At the point when she felt her lungs would burst, Travis stopped and pulled her into what she thought at first was a tangle of downed trees. On closer examination, she saw they were sheltered in the remains of a crude log cabin, the kind a miner might have built over a hundred years before.

His arms encircled her, pulling her close. She rested her head against his chest, feeling the hard pounding of his heart, and some of her panic eased. "What are we going to do?" she whispered.

"We're going to rest here for a minute," he said. "We'll see if they're following us."

"They'll be able to tell where we crashed through the woods," she said. "They'll know we're in here."

"Most people aren't trained trackers," he said. "None of their shots hit us because they weren't aiming—they were just firing wildly in our general direction."

They had gotten lucky this time. But what about next time? "If they trap us in here, how long can we hold them off?"

"We have maybe thirty rounds of ammunition for the Ruger, less for the Glock."

"So not long."

"That rifle the blond guy was toting will rip through this old wood like tacks through paper," he said. "If they get close enough, how much ammo we have left won't matter."

"You do know how to reassure a woman."

"Is that what you want? Pretty lies to make you feel better?"

"No. Thank you for being honest with me." They had always told each other the truth—until she lied to him about Duane. In trying to save him, she had destroyed so much. "I could offer to surrender if they let you go," she said. "You heard what those two men said—Duane wants me alive."

"Because he loves you so much." He spoke the words with a sneer.

"Because he loves that he can control me. Or he could. Getting away from him, running for our lives here in the wilderness, has shown me what I can do. I won't stay with him again. But I'll make him think I will if it will give you time to get away."

His arms tightened around her. "No. I won't let him or his men have you. Now be quiet and try to rest. We need to listen for them."

She settled against him, but her mind raced, preventing rest. The odds that Duane would let Travis go in exchange for her were slim, but with Travis's cooperation they might be able to trick him. The tough part would be distracting the hunters he had sent out after them. Maybe she could draw their fire here in the ruined cabin while Travis sneaked out the back and circled behind them. Did they have enough ammunition to make that plan feasible? And what about his assertion that the rifle bullets would cut through the old wood as if it weren't there? Her stomach churned along with her thoughts, a stew of frustration. She hated feeling helpless like this.

Travis slipped his arm from around her shoulder and leaned forward. "Listen," he hissed.

Something—or someone—was moving through the underbrush and not bothering to disguise the sound of his approach. Travis put his eye to a gap between the logs, and she found a gap to peer through also. At first, she saw nothing. Then she detected a shaking in the trees. The blond young man emerged, rifle at the ready.

"Come out with your hands up and we won't shoot," he shouted, and her blood turned to ice.

Travis gripped her wrist, whether in reassurance or restraint, she couldn't tell.

"We know you're here," the young man shouted. "You won't get away." But he had turned his back to them, aiming his words at the general surroundings. She exchanged a glance of relief with Travis. Blondie hadn't seen their hiding place—not yet.

The older man emerged from the woods to the west, his face flushed, his breath coming in pants. "Did you find them?" he gasped.

Blondie shook his head. "They came this way though. I'm sure of it." He scuffed at the leaf mold at his feet. "It's too dry for tracks. What about Will and Jacko? You heard from them?"

"They're doing a sweep away from the river. No sign of anything yet."

"They couldn't have gone far," Blondie said,

scanning the area. "No one could in this thick underbrush."

"Come on. They're headed for the bridge." The older man slapped him on the back. "They'll try to catch the train. We'll have them then."

Together, the two men moved away. Leah leaned back against the rough log wall and closed her eyes. For long minutes, neither she nor Travis said anything.

Travis was the first to rouse himself. He moved back to the gap in the logs. "We should keep an eye out for Will and Jacko," he said. "Do you know them?"

"No. But I didn't know the names of a lot of men who worked for Duane. And most of them didn't know my name, either. I was just—the woman." Or "Duane's woman" or one of the other names he called her when he was in a bad mood. She had learned to ignore the name-calling and even most of the physical abuse, turning her mind to other things while he ranted at her, or when he dragged her to his bedroom. Pretending not to be there was a coping mechanism.

But his reminders of how much control he had over her had hurt. When he wanted to get to her, he told her he planned to burn down the family cabin she had signed over to him. Or he told her the car that was still in her name was being used to run drugs down near the Texas border, or that he had spent the money her father left her to buy weapons and bombs.

"He'll have an army waiting for us at the bridge," she said. "We'll never get past them."

"No," he agreed. "They would spot us long before we got there."

"We could go back the way we came, try to make it to a road. They won't expect that." A fresh wave of despair washed over her at the idea of another two or three days in the wilderness, trying to survive on roots and berries.

"My guess is he has people watching the roads, too."

She buried her face in her hands. To find their way to a road, only to be stopped again, was too horrible to contemplate.

"You know Braeswood better than I do," Travis said. "What do you think is going through his mind right now?"

Braeswood's mind was not a sewer she wanted to explore. "I don't really care what he's thinking," she said. "Except that he's probably enraged that we've evaded him so far."

"If we can figure out what his next move is likely to be, we can try to get a step ahead of him," Travis said.

She pondered the idea, reviewing everything she had learned about Duane Braeswood in the past six months. "He's definitely a control freak," she said. "He spends a lot of time planning his operations, as he calls them. He drills everyone and oversees every detail. He brags about never having been caught because he's so meticulous."

"What does he do when something happens that he can't control?" Travis asked.

"You mean like the Feds raiding his home and me running away? He blows up. He does exactly what he's done this time—he throws every resource at the problem."

"Would you say he acts irrationally?"

She considered this. "Not irrationally, exactly. But his reaction is over the top. Out of proportion."

"But he tries to think of every possible angle to solve the problem?" Travis frowned.

"Not exactly, no. He's really smart, but he's arrogant, too. He decides what the problem is, then what the solution is and goes all out to use that solution to fix the problem."

"So he might overlook something."

"He might. But he really is a genius, I think. I don't remember him ever being wrong about a situation."

"No one can be right all the time," Travis said.

"No. But he has a lot of information and resources at his disposal."

"Even so, arrogance is a flaw we can exploit." He settled back against the logs once more, hands resting on his knees. "I'm guessing he's a man who enjoys luxury. That wasn't some little cabin in the woods he was renting."

"Of course. He can afford it."

"He doesn't like being uncomfortable. He doesn't like roughing it here in the woods."

She snorted. "Trust me, he's not roughing it. If he was in that group we saw headed up the trail, you can bet the others are carrying most of his load, and he'll have the best of everything in his campsite."

"He's called off the search every night."

"We can't count on him doing that tonight. Not when he knows we're so close."

"Still, even with night-vision goggles, it's not easy stumbling around in these woods, especially with a bunch of gear. Better to station sentries along the approach to the bridge and wait for us to come to them."

"Which means we're still trapped."

"Blondie and the older guy only mentioned two other men by name. That's four, plus maybe Braeswood."

"Duane would have at least one man with him as a bodyguard. Probably Eddie Roland."

"So that's seven. I counted eight on the trail when we first spotted them. Eight men can guard the bridge pretty effectively, but they can't guard the whole river."

A shiver of apprehension raced up her spine. "What are you suggesting?"

"The railroad follows the course of the river through the wilderness area," he said. "We can cross anywhere and hit the tracks. Then we lie low until the train approaches and we flag it down."

She stared at him, digesting this information.

"You don't think it's a good idea?" he said.

"We can't just wade across the river," she said. "The water is flowing really fast and it's bound to be ice cold. It's probably deep, too. I mean, there's a reason there's a bridge to the hiking trail. A really big bridge. And getting to the river anyplace but at the bridge is going to be tough. It's in a gorge. The banks are really steep."

"That's why Braeswood won't expect us to attempt it. But there's bound to be a place we can climb down. An animal trail we can follow.

And this time of year the water is at its lowest point. We can get across. We're both strong swimmers."

"I can swim laps in a pool," she said. "That's a lot different from swimming an ice-cold, raging river. Especially when we haven't had a decent meal in three days."

"Then you can wait on the bank while I go across and get help," he said. He leaned over and took her hand. "This is our best chance of getting to safety. We can't afford to wait much longer."

He was right. She had already done so many things in the past six months that she never would have thought she was capable of. What was climbing down a cliff and swimming across a cold, raging river when compared to all that? And if they did die in the attempt, it was better than being gunned down by one of Duane's thugs, or worse, going back to Duane. "I'm willing to try," she said. "But you're not going to leave me behind. We'll do this together."

He pulled her close and kissed her. When he released her, he was almost smiling. "The moon is almost full," he said. "That will help us."

"What does the moon have to do with any of this?"

"We'll have to make the crossing at night," he said. "It will lessen our chances of being spotted, in case they're patrolling the bank or scanning it with binoculars."

"So we're going to climb down cliffs and swim the river at night?"

He patted her shoulder. "You can do it."

Right. Maybe she had made a mistake being so stalwart through this whole ordeal. Now he thought she was a superhero!

Chapter Thirteen

Travis didn't need Leah's incredulous look to tell him that what he proposed was crazy. But, as the saying went, desperate times called for desperate measures. "The best chance we have to get away from here safely is to do something Braeswood thinks is impossible," he said. "Yes, the river is cold and the water is fast, but it's not that wide—about the length of the pool back in our gym in DC. I'm not saying it will be easy, but I don't think it's impossible."

The long, mournful wail of a train whistle

echoed through the canyon. "There goes our ride," Leah said, a stricken look on her face.

Travis powered up the phone and checked the time. "Eleven fifteen. Now we know what time we need to be at the track tomorrow."

"I thought you said we're crossing at night."

"We are. We'll cross the river at night to lessen the chance of our being seen. Once we reach the other side, we'll have to lie low until right before the train comes. We can't risk one of Braeswood's men spotting us."

"What will happen after we leave here?" she asked. "To Braeswood, I mean?"

"We'll mobilize a team to move into this area. If we're lucky, we'll get to Braeswood and his men before they realize you and I are gone. With the evidence we've collected already and your testimony, we should be able to put them away for a very long time."

"Do you think the court will believe me?"

"They will." He squeezed her hand. "I believe you."

"You didn't at first."

"I was angry." He shifted to face her. "I let my pride get in the way of what I knew in my heart. When I read your note the day you left, I should have realized something was wrong. I should have followed up and done more to protect you."

She lightly touched the back of his hand. "I wanted you to stay away. If you had come after me, Duane would have killed you. I couldn't save Sarah, but at least I could save you."

"I'd rather have taken my chances and still had you."

She sat back and closed her eyes. "I want to forget about everything that happened, but it's not easy."

"When we get out of here, you should talk to

a counselor or a therapist," he said. "Someone who can help."

"Maybe we both should."

He hesitated, then nodded. He wasn't the type to unload his problems on someone else, but his feelings about what had happened to Leah were in such turmoil, maybe talking to a professional would help him sort them out. "That's a good idea," he said. "Maybe we can help each other."

His first instinct was to leap in and fix everything for her, but he understood that in this case, charging in and taking over wasn't going to help. He had to navigate a tightrope between her desire for independence and his need to protect her. "Try to get some rest," he said. "We'll stay here another hour or two, then start walking. We'll try to pick out a place to cross the river while we still have light, then wait until full dark to set out."

She made a small noise of assent, then lay

down on her side, her back to him. He leaned back against the logs, the loaded gun beside him, and tried to sleep. They would both need every bit of strength they could muster to get through the night.

THOUGH LEAH HAD slept for over an hour, she didn't feel refreshed by the rest. Disjointed, confusing dreams had plagued her—dreams of running from unseen enemies, or of being trapped in houses with many rooms but no exits. Travis had been in the dreams as well, as a face at the window outside the house, or a voice calling her name. But they were never able to reach each other as she struggled through the dream world.

When she opened her eyes he was watching her. "You were restless," he said. "I thought you were having a nightmare. I wanted to wake you, but I wasn't sure if that was the right thing to do."

She sat and tried to straighten her rumpled clothing. "I read somewhere that dreams are the subconscious trying to solve problems."

"So, did your dream give you any solutions?"

"Not yet. But I can be patient." She glanced out the gap between the logs, at the long shadows of tree trunks stretched across the forest floor. "When can we leave here?" she asked.

"Whenever you're ready."

"Then let's go now." As much as she dreaded the ordeal that lay ahead, she was ready to get it over with.

They left the log ruins and began hiking along the bluff. They headed upstream, staying out of sight of the riverbank itself, but always keeping the sound of the river to their right. They hiked for two hours—what she judged to be four or five miles—then cautiously made their way to the edge of the bluff and looked down on the water. They had been steadily climbing all afternoon, so she wasn't surprised to see the water lay some forty feet below. The setting sun silvered the water where it tumbled over rocks in the narrow channel, but the bank they stood on was already in shadow.

"How are we ever going to get down there?" she asked.

"We'll have to walk along the bank until we find a less steep place or an animal path or something."

He sounded so confident that there would be a less steep place or a path. "What if it just gets steeper?" she asked.

His eyes met hers, calm but determined. "Then we'll walk in the other direction."

Right. What else could they do? She followed him upstream for another half hour, scanning the steep embankment but seeing nothing that looked promising. Bunches of drying grass and a scattering of yellow and purple wildflowers

clung to the reddish soil that had collected between the rocks. The embankment on the oppo-
site side of the river, leading up to the railroad
tracks, looked just as steep and forbidding.

Travis stopped, and she almost stumbled into
him. "I think we can get down here," he said.

She stood on tiptoe to peer over his shoulder
and studied the faint line of what might have
been a trail, snaking down the slope at a sharp
angle. "You're kidding."

"We can do it," he said. "We'll take it slow and
use our walking sticks to help balance."

She shivered, as much from fear as from the
chill that descended with the setting sun. "What
do you think made that trail?" she asked.

"Mountain goats, maybe. Deer? Some kind of
animals headed to the river for water."

"Maybe you need four legs to get down something like that," she said.

"You climbed down a mountain yesterday. You can do this."

Right. The whole superpower thing again. They were going to have to have a talk about that sometime, but maybe not now.

"We'll wait for the moon to rise," he said. "Then we'll head down." He moved back toward the cover of trees. "In the meantime, we'll find a place to wait."

"You can wait. I'm going to find food." She turned and started walking back the way they'd come.

"Where are you going?" he asked.

"Some of those bushes we passed earlier looked like raspberries." The idea of anything to eat made her mouth water.

He fell into step beside her. When they reached the cluster of bushes again, her heart sank. Combing through the branches, all they found were a few shriveled berries. They ate the dozen or so bruised fruits, then she plucked some rose hips from the wild rosebushes that grew nearby. "If we had a fire, we could heat water and make raspberry leaf tea," she said, though she couldn't muster much enthusiasm for the idea.

"We can't risk it." He plucked a leaf from a raspberry bush and chewed, then spit it out. "It tastes terrible."

Her laughter surprised her; she hadn't thought she had any mirth left in her. "The look on your face is priceless," she said.

He made a show of looking around them. "What else do you think I should try? Fir branches?" He grabbed hold of a nearby evergreen branch. "Is the tree bark any good? I've heard this place serves an excellent stone soup."

"You'll have to settle for chewing gum." She handed him a stick from the packet she had unearthed earlier in the day. She had been saving it for right before they set out on their river crossing, but now seemed a better time. "I'd forgotten I had this in my pocket."

The gum did little to satisfy their hunger, but the act of chewing and the little bit of sweetness the gum provided felt good. Travis took her hand. "Come on. Let's find a place near that trail to wait for moonrise. And try to watch where you step. We don't want to go tumbling off the cliff."

"That would be one way to get to the bottom quickly."

"Come on, you." He tugged her alongside him and squeezed her shoulders.

They moved a little farther into the woods and settled down against the large trunk of a towering fir, the air perfumed with the Christmas tree scent. "You might as well take another nap," he said, patting his thigh.

She hesitated, then stretched out beside him, her head in his lap. He idly stroked her hair and she remembered another summer afternoon when they had sat like this, on the National Mall, listening to a free concert of classical music. Had it really only been last summer? It seemed a lifetime ago. "This is kind of romantic," she said. "If you overlook the fact that I'd kill for a steak and a shower."

He laughed. "I guess it is—if you overlook those things." He caressed her shoulder. "It's good to see you in a better mood."

"I guess I've still got some fight left in me."

"Good. I have a feeling you're going to need it."

She closed her eyes and snuggled against him. "Bring it on," she said, already sinking toward sleep.

SHE WOKE WITH a start when Travis nudged her. "It's time to go," he said, his voice low.

She sat and brushed pine needles from her

clothes, then glanced toward the bluff, and the indentation that marked the beginning of the steep path they had to negotiate to the river. The moon shone like a white spotlight above the trees, bathing everything in a silvery glow.

"Are you ready?" Travis extended his hand.

She took it and let him pull her to her feet. "Probably not," she said. "But sitting here longer isn't going to make me any more ready."

He handed her the stout walking stick she had been using since they had come down off the mountain. "Use this to steady yourself on the way down. If you feel your feet slipping out from under you, sit down right away."

"I'll do that. And pray. A lot."

"That's a good idea, too."

They set out, picking their way down the narrow, steep path. A chill breeze buffeted them, but Leah scarcely noticed, she was focused so intently on placing each step.

In front of her, Travis froze. "What is it?" she asked, her voice a hoarse whisper.

"Look." He pointed and she shifted her gaze some distance ahead of them and to the right. Her breath caught as she stared at a large black bear making its way down to the water, two chubby cubs ambling along after her. The cubs batted at each other and tumbled around their mother's feet. The mother hefted her big body over rocks and around tree trunks, looking back to check on the twins from time to time.

"She doesn't know we're here," Leah whispered.

"We're downwind from her."

"The babies are adorable, but I'm just as glad we didn't meet them in the woods."

"Me, too." He turned his attention away from the bears to her. Moonlight softened and shadowed his features, like a smudged charcoal portrait. "How are you doing?"

"Okay," she said. "The climb down isn't as bad as I feared. The mountain was worse." She glanced toward the river. The rushing current had provided the background noise for much of their day, but the sound was louder now, and the moonlight cast an eerie glow over the foaming rapids. How were they ever going to get across that?

As if reading her mind, Travis said, "We'll walk upstream a ways, and cross where the current isn't as swift."

"I hope Duane and his men aren't watching us." She shivered at the thought.

"If they were, we would have heard from them by now."

"I guess when it comes to Duane and his buddies, no news really is good news."

They continued down the slope. The mother bear and her cubs reached the river, then meandered downstream. "Maybe she's looking for a better place to cross, too," Leah said.

"Maybe she is."

They reached the narrow strip of gravel beside the water. The sound was much louder here, so that they had to raise their voices to talk over it. "Which way do we go?" she asked.

"I think I saw calmer water downstream."

If not for the danger, this would have been a romantic scene, strolling in the light of the full moon along the riverbank, silvery cliffs towering overhead, silvery water dancing alongside. The rapids gave way to a smoother, though wider and possibly deeper stretch of water. "I think this is the place," Travis said. He slipped off the pack and began unbuttoning his shirt.

"What are you doing?" she asked.

"It's cool enough that if we stand around in wet clothing after we cross, we risk hypothermia. We'll be better off if we wrap our clothes in plastic in the pack and put them on again when we reach the other side." He peeled off the shirt and unzipped his pants, then bent to untie the laces of his hiking boots.

"Okay." Undressing made sense. But the prospect of crossing the river naked made her feel even more weak and vulnerable.

"Come on," he said. "I want to get this over with."

Reluctantly, she began to strip off her clothing. She turned her back to him, though why, she didn't know. It wasn't as if he'd never seen her naked before. The night air raised goose bumps on her skin as she folded her clothing into a compact bundle.

When she turned around to hand her clothing and shoes to Travis, his gaze was fixed on her. "You should see yourself in the moonlight," he said, his voice husky with emotion. "You're so beautiful."

She couldn't look directly at him, afraid her face would give away all the emotion she was feeling—fear and love and shame and wonder. She watched him out of the corner of her eye and noted the way the moonlight burnished the muscles of his shoulders and arms. The bullet wound on his ribs was still an angry red, but the scar somehow highlighted the beauty of the rest of him—the flat abdomen and muscular thighs, and the thick perfection of his sex.

In this deserted wilderness, bathed in silvery moonlight beside the flowing waters of the river, they might have been Adam and Eve in paradise. Except that they were about to risk their lives crossing that river, and while the moonlight would help guide them, it would also make them more visible to anyone who might be watching.

"Are you afraid?" she asked, blurting the question she had only meant to think to herself.

"Yes," he said. "Any sane person would be. But we're going to do this anyway."

She nodded. "Yes. We're going to do this."

He wrapped the clothing, along with both guns and the ammunition, in the pack's rain fly and then in the plastic trash bag, then lashed the pack shut. "That should keep everything dry," he said. "As long as I don't lose the pack."

"Don't you dare." The thought of having to flag down the train naked made her face heat.

He laughed. "I promise, I'll hang on to the pack. Come here." He pulled her close.

He was warm and solid—and aroused. "Now isn't the time for this," she said, even as she felt her skin heat and her nipples bead into tight peaks.

He nuzzled her neck. "I know, but the sight of you naked in the moonlight definitely turns me on."

And the feel of him naked against her did the

same for her. "Save that thought for later." She reluctantly pulled out of his embrace and faced the water. "So what do you think? Just dive in?"

"Wade in. Use the walking stick to brace yourself. If you fall, let the current carry you downstream until you can regain your footing or swim. Aim your feet downstream and watch for obstacles."

"You talk as if you've done this kind of thing before," she said.

"I had to take a water rescue course once, in preparation for a mission." He cut his eyes to her. "Don't ask."

"I wouldn't dream of it." When they had started dating, she had adhered to a policy of not asking about his work with the Bureau. She didn't want to know what kind of danger he put himself in daily.

He took her hand and pulled her forward.

"You go first," he said. "That way I can see if you get in trouble and try to help."

"What if you get in trouble?" she asked.

"I promise to yell loudly." He pulled her tight against him and kissed her, a surprisingly fierce, passionate gesture. "It's going to be all right," he said.

"You're just saying that."

"I don't lie, remember?"

"I remember." She touched her fingers to his lips, then waded into the water.

The shock of the cold stole her breath and forced out an involuntary yelp. She faltered.

"Keep moving," Travis urged, stepping into the water behind her. "The faster you move, the sooner it will all be over."

She nodded, and forced herself to take a shaky step forward, and then another. The icy water pushed against her legs and the gravel river bottom continually shifted beneath her feet, making it difficult to keep her footing. It was so cold. How did those people who took polar bear plunges for charity or for fun ever do it? She planted the walking stick and held on tightly, clenching her teeth against the cold and shaking.

A few more steps and the water was up to mid-thigh, and then up to her hips. Fighting the current, she struggled forward, planting her foot on a smooth rock, bracing with the stick…

Then she was down, water engulfing her, cutting off the scream that ripped from her throat. The cold water rushed over her head and stole her breath, and rocks scraped her backside and arms.

She tried to stand, managing to get her head above water and sucking in a gasping breath. But the current made it impossible to find purchase on the rocky river bottom and her feet continually slipped out from under her. Remembering Travis's advice, she fought to turn her body and aim downstream as the river pulled her along. She popped to the surface again, gasping and shouting for help. Though who would hear besides Travis, she couldn't imagine.

She tried to relax and let the current carry her, focusing her efforts on keeping her head above water, but the constant buffeting against rocks and tree branches sticking up from the river bottom made that impossible. She feared she would be battered to death before she ever reached the shore.

Desperate, she grabbed hold of one jutting branch and clung to it as the water rushed around her. She was too weak to pull herself out of the water, but the momentary pause allowed her to catch her breath and assess her situation.

She was little more than halfway across the river, and at least a hundred yards past the point where she had fallen. She ached with the cold and her fingers were so numb she had trouble keeping hold of the branch she clung to. How long did it take for someone to die of hypothermia? An hour, or only minutes? She raised her head as far out of the water as she could, and spotted Travis standing in midstream, water to his chest, looking down the river. Relief flooded her at the sight of him. At least the water hadn't dragged him under. After she rested here a moment, she would attempt to cross the rest of the way. Soon they would be together on the shore. She raised her hand and waved to let him know she was all right.

In that moment, the branch broke, sending her hurtling into the current once more.

Chapter Fourteen

"No!" The cry of frustration tore from Travis's throat as the current ripped Leah from her anchor. Exhausted and trembling with cold, he'd stopped halfway across the river to get his bearings and had been relieved to see her safe, clinging to the branch of a tree that had lodged in the riverbed a hundred yards downstream. Now anger and fear gave him renewed strength and he dived into the water and started stroking for the far shore. The current carried him downstream, but he kept his eye on his goal and fought to make headway. After another minute his feet struck the bottom and he waded forward, pushing hard.

He didn't allow himself a moment of rest when he climbed out of the water, but ran downstream, in the direction Leah had disappeared. He feared at first he had lost her. "Leah!" he shouted as he ran, scanning the tumbling water for some sign of her dark hair or flailing limbs. The thundering roar of the rapids swallowed up the cry.

He spotted her twenty yards ahead. She was swimming, but making little headway, clearly tiring in her fight against the rapids. He ran farther up the bank, shedding the pack as he moved. Leaving it beside the water, he strode into the icy current once more, setting a course to intercept Leah.

He was still ten yards away from her when she went under and didn't resurface. "Leah, no!" he shouted, and barreled toward her. He plunged under the water at the place he thought she had gone down, but found nothing but the gravel bottom.

He surfaced to take a breath, then dived, again and again, until his teeth chattered violently and fatigue dragged at his limbs. On the verge of giving up, something bumped against his leg— something soft and pale. He reached down and his hand closed around Leah's ankle.

He dived and gathered her body close and dragged her to the surface. Eyes shut, she lay limp in his arms. Not allowing himself to think, he wrapped his arm around her in a lifesaving carry and began fighting his way back to the shore, his body and mind numb to everything but the goal of saving her.

It took every last reserve of energy to struggle up the bank, dragging Leah with him. He lay with his face in the mud just out of the water, shivering, his heart thudding. He turned his head to look at her, her pale skin tinted blue in the moonlight.

"No," he said again. He forced himself up onto his hands, then he crawled to her and put his ear to her chest, listening for her heartbeat. He thought he heard a faint pulse. He pressed his cheek to her lips and felt a faint flutter of warm air. Quickly, he turned her onto her side and began rubbing her back, then chafing her wrists and hands. "Come on, Leah," he pleaded. "Wake up for me."

She jerked and coughed, then convulsed as she vomited up a flood of murky liquid. He held her, brushing her hair out of her face. "That's a girl," he said. "Get it all up. You're going to be all right."

"Travis." The single word was barely audible, but it hit him with the impact of a shout. He helped her sit up and she stared at him, blinking. "Wh…what happened?"

"The branch you were clinging to must have broken," he said. "The current pulled you under."

She curled her knees to her chest and wrapped her arms around them. "I'm so cold."

"Let me warm you up." He pulled her to him, then they lay together, legs and arms wrapped around each other, until her shivering subsided.

"You saved me," she said after a long while.

"I thought I'd lost you." Seeing her slip under the water had been the worst moment of his life. He shuddered, remembering.

"No. Not yet." She burrowed her head against his shoulder. "I'm so cold."

"We should get some clothes on."

"Where's the pack?"

"I left it on the bank when I dived in after you." He looked up and spotted the pack, sitting fifty yards upstream. Exhaustion pulled at him. It might as well have been a mile away.

"One of us is going to have to get it," she said.

"I know." He heaved himself into a sitting position. "I'll get it."

He retrieved the pack and dropped it beside her, then fell to his knees. He took out one of the water bottles and drank, then handed it to her while he opened the pack. Relief rushed through him as he unfolded the plastic. "Everything is dry," he said.

They dressed quickly. The clothing felt good against his skin. Warmer, though not really warm enough.

"Maybe we should build a fire," he said.

"A fire sounds heavenly." She looked down the riverbank, toward the bridge and the train station, too far to see from their vantage point. "But we probably shouldn't risk it. If Duane and his men found us now, I wouldn't have the energy to run away from them."

"You're right." He shouldered the pack. "Let's find someplace safe to wait until morning and wrap up in the space blanket. Our body heat will warm us."

A few hundred yards upstream, they found a hollowed-out place in the bank half hidden by brush and weeds. They crawled into this and pulled the space blanket around them. Within minutes they had fallen into an exhausted sleep.

LEAH WOKE TO bright light hitting her face. She moaned and tried to turn away from the painful glare, but there was no room in her cramped hiding place. "I was going to wake you soon." Travis spoke from a few feet away, where he knelt before the pack. "The train will be here in a half hour or so."

The train. Their salvation. But to reach it, they had to climb the steep bank to the tracks. Every inch of her ached at the prospect. She pushed aside the space blanket. "How are we going to get the train to stop?" she asked.

"I thought we'd use your sweater as a flag," he said. "It's red, so they'll be able to see it from a long way off."

"My sweater?" She clutched at the garment in question. "You want me to flag down the train topless?"

He grinned. "I'll bet the engineer would stop for that."

At her horrified look, he laughed. "You can wear the fleece jacket. It zips up the front. And once we're on board, you can have the sweater back."

She couldn't think of a solid argument against this plan, so she reluctantly peeled off the sweater and handed it over. While she put on the fleece and zipped it up, he tied the arms of the sweater to a tree branch and waved it experimentally.

"This ought to work. I'll stand on the track and wave it over my head."

"What if the engineer doesn't see you? What if he can't stop in time to avoid hitting you?"

"I remember now. You always were a grouch before you had your morning coffee."

She glared at him.

"The train isn't traveling that fast," he said. "I'll stand where I'm sure the engineer can see me from a long way off." He tugged the space blanket from around her and began folding it. "Are you ready?"

"I just need to shower, brush my teeth, comb my hair and do my makeup, and have some breakfast." She combed her hair back out of her face with her fingers. "Oh, wait. I can't do any of those things."

"There will be food on the train," he said. "And coffee. And restrooms."

"You sure know how to tempt a girl." She shoved herself up. "I'm ready."

He shouldered the pack, then led the way up

the steep bank. The trail was straight up, and slippery with gravel, but she managed to pull herself up by gritting her teeth and picturing the cheeseburger she was going to devour as soon as they reached whatever passed for a dining car on the tourist train.

At the top of the trail, Travis put his hand on her shoulder. "Listen."

She stilled, and the low moan of the train whistle reached her ears. Her heart leaped. "It's coming."

He removed the pack and handed it to her, took the flag he had made from her sweater, and walked out onto the track. The slim rails were only thirty-six inches apart, coarse gravel filling in the space between the ties.

The train appeared around a bend up ahead, the engine a black monster, wheels churning, white steam pouring from the smokestack and shooting out from the brakes as the engineer negotiated the curve. Sunlight glinted off the engine's windows, making it impossible to see the engineer. The whistle sounded again, much louder now and more urgent.

Both hands raised over his head, Travis waved the makeshift flag. The train's brakes squealed, shooting out steam, and gradually the engine slowed. Travis joined Leah beside the tracks. Behind the coal car, passengers leaned out of the window to gape at the man and woman beside the tracks. "We must look like a couple of derelicts," Leah said, aware of her unwashed body, messy hair, and torn and dirty clothing. Travis sported a four-day growth of beard and equally ragged clothing.

"They'll just think we're a couple of backpackers." He took the pack from her and slung it onto his back. "Nothing that unusual out here."

"What do we do when it stops?" she asked, as the train rolled slowly toward them.

"I'll show them my credentials." He dug the folder with his badge and identification from his pants pocket.

She slid her hand into his. Now that they were so close to safety—to food and hot water and an end to the physical and mental exhaustion of being pursued by killers—her whole body vibrated with anticipation. She focused on the engine's wheels churning slowly down the track. The engineer leaned out of the window toward them, checking them out. Travis held up his credentials, though Leah doubted the engineer could make out anything about the wallet from this distance.

The engine drew alongside them, the sound of the whistle deafening. Leah covered her ears and moved closer to the tracks, ready to climb on board as soon as the engine stopped. She couldn't see into the cab anymore, though she could hear some of the passengers shouting questions about the reason for the delay. Any second now, they would be on board. Safe.

Then, instead of stopping, the train began moving faster. Fast enough that instead of walking, they had to trot to keep up with it. "Hey!" Travis shouted. "Stop! We need help!"

A stern-faced man in the blue suit and billed cap of a conductor appeared on the steps of the platform leading to the first car behind the coal tender. "You have to board at the station," he shouted above the hiss of steam and the churn of the engine's wheels.

"We need help!" Travis protested.

The conductor shook his head and pointed downstream, in the direction the train had come, toward the Needleton Station. Where Duane and his men were no doubt waiting for them.

TRAVIS AND LEAH STOPPED. Frustration and rage boiled inside him. After all they had been through, this was too much. He grabbed Leah's arm. "Come on," he said. "We're going to have to jump on board."

"What?" But she kept pace with him as he ran toward the cars at the rear of the train. Though the engine had picked up speed, it still wasn't moving more than a few miles an hour. He watched the cars as he passed, trying to judge the distance between the track and the bottom step leading up to the platform at the rear of each car. It was a big leap, but if he could make it, he could help Leah up after him.

Catcalls and abuse assailed them as they ran. An empty plastic cup bounced off his shoulder. "They're not going to let us on!" Leah called.

Travis stopped and held up his credentials. "FBI!" he shouted. "Let us board."

"Hazel, I think that badge might be real," one man said to the wide-eyed woman beside him.

A few hands reached out to Travis from the

platform. He leaped, his toe just catching the step, and they hauled him on board, then he turned to help Leah. Two other men leaned out to assist, and together they pulled her up onto the platform.

The other passengers bombarded them with questions. Who were they and what were they doing flagging down the train? Was he really an FBI agent? Why was the FBI all the way out here? They pressed forward to examine the badge and identification Travis displayed, and stared at the disheveled, dirty pair as if they were from another planet.

"Maybe it's a movie," someone farther back in the car said. "Or a television show."

A conductor—maybe the same one who had glared at them from behind the coal tender—pushed his way through the crowd at the back of the car. "Let me see those credentials," he demanded, extending his hand.

Travis handed over the wallet. The conductor studied the picture, then Travis's face. "This doesn't look much like you," he said.

"It looks like me when I haven't spent four days in the wilderness." He took back the wallet and returned it to his pocket. "I've been pursuing a fugitive."

The conductor nodded to Leah, who stood at Travis's elbow. "What about her? Is she an agent, too?"

"She's a key witness in my case," he said.

"What I am is half starved," she said. "Does this train have a dining car?"

"The refreshment car is through here." The conductor turned and they followed him up the aisle. The other passengers gaped at them with open curiosity, the spectacular scenery outside the windows momentarily forgotten.

At the end of the car, Leah stopped before a door marked Ladies. "I'm just going to go in here for a minute," she said. She held out her hand. "May I have my sweater, please?"

"The refreshment car is next," the conductor said. "You can meet us there."

She nodded. "Are you sure?" Travis asked as he handed over the sweater, which was still attached to the tree branch.

Her smile burned through him. "Don't worry. I'm not going to let you get too far away from me again. I'll meet you there in a few minutes. Go ahead and order me a cheeseburger."

Travis followed the conductor across the platforms into the next car, which contained a snack bar manned by two young women in bib overalls. The aroma of coffee and grilled food made him feel a little faint, and it took all his willpower to wait for the couple in front of him to finish before he placed his order.

"You must be really hungry," the young woman said after he had asked for three burgers, two orders of fries, two milks, two coffees and a package of cookies.

"You have no idea," he said, and took out his wallet.

"What's this all about?" A third man joined Travis and the conductor at the snack bar. "Russell Waddell," he said. "Railroad security."

"Special Agent Travis Steadman." Travis displayed his creds, then accepted his change from the snack bar cashier.

"I'll have to ask you to surrender your gun until we get to Silverton," Waddell said. "The young lady, too, if she's armed. We don't allow weapons on the train."

"As a law officer, I'm licensed to carry a duty weapon," Travis said. He didn't bother mentioning the Glock Leah no doubt still carried tucked under the oversize fleece jacket.

"He says he's after a fugitive," the conductor volunteered.

"Here on this train?" Waddell's eyebrows rose.

"I've been tracking him through the Weminuche Wilderness," Travis said. He tore open one of the cartons of milk the young woman handed him and drank it down in a gulp. "As soon as we get into cell phone range, I'll call for backup."

"You won't have cell service until we reach Silverton in a little over an hour," Waddell said. Apparently he'd decided to drop the argument about Travis's gun. "But we have a radio you can use to relay a message to our headquarters in Durango."

"Great. As soon as Leah and I have a chance to eat we'll do that." He glanced toward the back of the car. What was taking her so long?

"She's probably in there cleaning up," the conductor said.

He nodded.

"Your order's ready, sir."

He turned to accept the tray of food.

"Here she comes," the conductor said.

Relief flooded him when he glanced back and saw Leah making her way toward him. But instead of returning his smile, she sent him a tense, worried look. He set down the tray and started toward her. "Leah, is something wrong?"

"Nothing wrong at all."

Travis's mouth went dry when he recognized the man who spoke. Walking very close to Leah, his arm around her, Duane Braeswood offered a smile with no mirth. Instinctively, Travis reached for the gun at his waistband.

"Good to see you again, Agent Steadman," Braeswood said. "Leah and I were just discussing what a coincidence it is that we should all end up on this train."

Chapter Fifteen

Leah's eyes pleaded with Travis for help. He eased his hand away from his weapon. The way Braeswood held Leah, he probably had a gun or knife pressed against her. So much for the rule about no weapons on the train.

"Friend of yours?" Waddell asked. He had probably picked up on Travis's hostility.

Travis forced himself to relax. "We've known each other a long time," he said, trying to sound casual.

"You might say we were once rivals for the affections of a certain beautiful woman." The smile Braeswood gave Leah made Travis's skin crawl.

Leah licked her lips, her eyes glassy with terror. "Duane says he has a private car we can wait in until we reach Durango," she said, her voice strained with tension.

"That's right," Duane said. "Bring your food with you and we'll catch up on old times."

"What about the call you needed to make?" Waddell asked. "The radio is in the engine compartment."

"Making a call like that through a third party could jeopardize national security," Duane said. "Not to mention compromise Ms. Carlisle's safety."

Leah's expression grew more pained. Travis wanted to punch the smirk off Braeswood's face. Waddell wasn't likely to buy a phony excuse like "national security," but for Leah's sake, Travis was going to have to sell the idea. "The guy I'm after isn't going anywhere in a hurry," he said to Waddell. "Rather than try to relay what I want through the people at railroad headquarters, it's probably a better idea to make the call myself when we get nearer Silverton."

Waddell frowned. "If you're sure."

"I'm sure." He picked up the tray and wondered if shoving the food in Duane's face would distract him enough to make him release Leah. But if Braeswood did have a gun in his hand, he might fire it, and gunfire in the crowded confines of the train was bound to result in innocent people getting hurt.

They made their way forward to a car marked Private—Reserved. "Hello, Mr. B." An attendant greeted them at the door.

"Marcie, these are my friends Leah and Travis," Braeswood said. "They're going to be riding with me the rest of the way."

"Yes, sir." The dark-haired young woman

flashed a friendly smile. "Welcome aboard. Can I get you anything to drink?"

"Water would be good." Travis followed Braeswood to a small dining table covered with an old-fashioned lace cloth.

"And you, ma'am?" Marcie asked.

"Water is fine." Leah slumped into a chair next to Travis. Braeswood withdrew the gun he had held pressed into her side, though he kept hold of it, resting it on his thigh beneath the table.

"As long as you cooperate, no one gets hurt," he said in a low voice. "Try anything and I'll kill her. And you, too."

Travis ignored the threat, his focus on Leah. He pushed the tray toward her. "We might as well eat," he said.

He thought at first she might refuse, but after a moment, she reached for a now-cold French fry. It didn't matter that the food was cold and not all that appetizing. He was so hungry he could have eaten almost anything. Braeswood said nothing while they finished the meal.

When they were done, Marcie cleared their trays, then returned to stand by the door. Travis leaned across the table and spoke in a low voice. "Whatever you're planning, you won't get away with it," he said.

"I was planning to return to Durango to gather more forces and equipment to hunt down the two of you," Braeswood said. "You've saved me that trouble and expense." He turned to Leah, frowning. "I must say, I'm very disappointed in you. I warned you what would happen if you tried to run away, and now you leave me no choice but to follow through on that promise of punishment."

She glared at him, saying nothing. The smile he gave her sent a fog of red through Travis's brain. It took every bit of his willpower and training not to leap across the table and attempt to rip that sneer from Braeswood's face. "You've wasted a lot of my time and cost me a great deal of money," Braeswood said. "So before I kill you I should try to recoup at least part of my losses. I have a friend who owns a brothel down near the Mexican border where a young woman like you would be in high demand."

Still Leah said nothing, but her face paled and her breathing grew more shallow. Travis sensed her retreating into herself, returning to that pale, frightened woman he had pulled from the car in the driveway of that rented mountain home only three days ago. "You'll never get away with it, Duane," he said, his voice as menacing as he could make it. "Even if you kill both of us, the rest of my team knows you're in this area and they will stop at nothing to hunt you down."

"The Feds are nothing but a bunch of half-trained foot soldiers strangling in red tape and government oversight." Braeswood met Travis's glare with a cool look. "I'll admit, you impressed me a little bit, the way you managed to evade my team back there in the wilderness. But they would have found you eventually, and then your exalted government agency would have pretended you didn't exist, or blamed your demise on your own clumsy efforts. If you're really so interested in seeing justice done in your lifetime, you'd join my organization. We could use a man with your skills."

"Your organization is a bunch of murderers and thieves."

A muscle at the corner of Braeswood's eye twitched, the only indication of any emotion on his part. "Change is difficult," he said. "Watch a butterfly emerging from a cocoon sometime and you'll see how much work and pain is involved. But those who persevere through the brutality will, like the butterfly, soar."

"What a pretty speech," Travis said. "Is that your favorite pep talk for the troops?"

"I do more than talk about change," Braeswood said. "I work to make it happen. Something you government types don't understand." He checked his watch, an ornate gold Rolex. "We should reach Silverton about one p.m," he said. "I'll have a car and driver waiting there. The town is very remote, and the countryside around there is filled with old mines and Jeep trails. I shouldn't have too much difficulty finding a place to dispose of your bodies."

As IF ALL his talk about exiling her to a Mexican brothel hadn't been enough to frighten Leah, Duane's boast about disposing of their bodies should have been enough to send her into a faint from sheer terror. When she had stepped out of the ladies' room and almost collided with him, she was sure she was hallucinating, mistaking some stranger for the man who had haunted her nightmares for months. Then she had felt the hard jab of a gun barrel biting into her side and heard his voice, his words chilling her more deeply than the river water ever could have. "Hello, Leah. It's so good to see you again."

The shock of seeing him on the train, when she was so sure they were finally safe, had left her momentarily catatonic, but all his boasts of working toward a better world, familiar as they were, had shaken her awake again. The past few days of struggling to survive in the wilderness had shocked her out of the paralyzing stupor she had been in ever since her sister's death. Duane counted on people fearing him. Their fear gave him most of his power, so almost everything he said and did was calculated to make them more afraid. Now that she could see so clearly what he was doing, she wouldn't let him manipulate her with his threats anymore. She had to fight back with everything she had.

The door at the end of the car opened and the conductor entered. "We'll be arriving in Silverton in about half an hour, folks," he said. "Make sure you have all your belongings with you when you depart the train. If you're making the return trip to Durango, listen for the train whistle around three o'clock. That's your signal to head back this way."

"My friends and I have decided to return to Durango by road," Duane said. "I have a driver waiting for us."

"Then thank you again for riding the Durango & Silverton Railway," the conductor said, his face bland. "I hope you enjoyed the trip."

"Yes, it was very enjoyable." Duane took Leah's hand. "Especially since it allowed me to reconnect with my dear friends."

Leah pulled her hand away and glared at him.

He was so evil—how else to account for the fact that the prospect of murdering her and Travis didn't upset him in the least. He spoke of his plans to dispose of them in the same tone he might use to describe an afternoon picnic. The conductor appeared not to notice her hostility. "There's still some great scenery between here and the Silverton station," he said. "We'll be passing through Elk Park, then directly after that we'll come to Deadwood Gulch. Quite the view there. The train will slow so you can take pictures if you want."

She waited until the conductor had moved on to the next car before she turned on Duane. "You can't think you'll get away with murdering us," she said. "Too many people will know we were with you."

"They'll know a man named David Beaverton, a successful plastics manufacturer from Ohio, was with you," he said, his demeanor as calm as ever. "If they try to find such a person, they'll learn he died last year."

"Did you have anything to do with his death?" Travis asked.

"He died of a brain aneurysm at age forty. He and I share the same body type and general coloring. I have a contact in vital records who keeps me informed of such useful persons."

"So you stole his identity," Travis said.

The train slowed to a crawl. Marcie approached their table. "Can I get you anything, Mr. B?" she asked.

"No, thank you," he said. "We won't be requiring anything else this trip. Feel free to leave us alone."

"I'm assigned to this car for the whole trip," she said. She glanced out the window. "Not much longer. We're at Elk Park. Sometimes the train stops here, if we have a hiker or someone like that who needs to get off. Most of the time we just crawl through so folks can take pictures of the old bridge."

What had the conductor said? Something about Deadwood Gulch being next on the list? Leah raised her eyes to find Travis's gaze fixed on her. She didn't have to read minds to know what he was thinking—if they didn't find a way to get away from Duane before they reached Silverton—and definitely before he hustled them into his car and drove off into the mountains—they could very well be dead before nightfall.

Rage filled her at the thought that they had endured so much—struggled so much—only to have Duane win in the end. She couldn't let that happen. She wouldn't sit here and not try to do something to save herself and Travis. She shoved back her chair and stood. "I need some air," she said, and headed toward the viewing platform at the rear of the car.

"You need to stay here until we reach Silverton." Duane leaned back, giving her a clear view of the gun in his hand.

"I'm just stepping out on the platform," she said, reaching for the sliding door that led outside. "I feel like I'm going to throw up." Even as she said the words, she braced for the impact of a bullet slamming into her. Duane didn't like it when she talked back, and being in a semi-public place was no guarantee that he wouldn't lash out at her.

"You poor thing." Marcie jumped up to pull open the door for her. "The motion of the train affects some people that way, especially after a big meal. The fresh air will help you feel better."

Maybe Duane was reluctant to shoot Marcie along with Leah. Or maybe he didn't want to alert the security agent, Waddell, when he was so close to making his escape. Whatever the reason, he didn't shoot Leah now, though he kept his hand on the pistol and the weapon pointed in her direction, even as both men scraped back their chairs and prepared to follow. Leah lurched out onto the platform and clung to the railing as the cars rocked from side to side over a rough stretch of track. She stared up at the jutting mountain peaks that looked as if they had been painted by an artist in love with color. Bright yellow cascades of waste rock streaked the steep red and purple slopes, the white of snow in the shaded valleys and on the highest peaks giving way to the scarlet and gold of aspen, the deep green of spruce and pine, and the rust-orange splotches of beetle-killed fir. The air smelled of cinders and smoke and rushed against her skin in a chill wind.

Travis moved in close behind her, his arm around her waist. "You okay?" he asked.

"No." There was nothing okay about having had the last six months of her life stolen by the man who had murdered her sister and many others. Duane had robbed her of the job she loved, the marriage she had dreamed of, the sister she had adored. He had taken her money, trashed her reputation, and turned her days and nights into a nightmare that would probably haunt her for the rest of her life. Getting rid of him wouldn't change any of that, but it might prevent other people from enduring the same misery.

"Get away from her." Duane shoved Travis out of the way and took his place behind Leah, the pistol once more driven painfully into her side. "Make one wrong move and I'll blow your guts out," he said. "It will be a horrible, painful death, I promise."

She turned her head to look at him, careful to make her expression soft and inviting. "You don't have to worry about me, Duane," she said. "I know when I've been beat. I'm only going to stand here and let my head clear and enjoy the scenery."

His eyes narrowed. "Go ahead and enjoy it all you want," he said. "It will be one of the last sights you see."

"It's so incredibly beautiful," she said. "And I can't get over all the gold mines that are still active up here."

"I haven't seen any gold mines," he said, his tone scoffing. Yet she didn't miss the greedy light in his eyes.

"There are lots of them," she said. "I read somewhere that with the price of gold going up so much, a lot of people are working small claims again and making money at it. You just have to look for the openings in the rocks. There's one up there." She pointed up the slope.

"I don't see anything," he said.

"Come stand on the other side of me." She indicated the space where a length of cable closed off the steps leading toward the track. When the train stopped, a conductor would unhook this cable and passengers could file down the steps. "Lean out just a little ways and look straight up the slope, just at the tree line." She demonstrated, angling her body over the cable and gazing up the slope.

Travis moved in behind her once more, his whole body tensed. "I see what you're talking about," he said. "That little wooden structure?"

"Right." She turned to Duane, who had moved to her other side and was leaning, though not very far, and squinting up at the rocks. "Do you see it?" she asked.

"No."

"Lean out more. You need to look at an angle to really see it."

He did as she suggested, one foot almost off the floor as he arched farther over the cable.

"That's it," Leah said. "Perfect." She caught Travis's eye and he nodded. She put a hand on Duane's back and gritted her teeth. She could do this. She could push him off the platform, if it meant saving her own life and Travis's.

Travis lunged forward and grabbed Duane's arm with his left hand. In his right, he held the Glock. "Duane Braeswood, you're under arrest," he said.

Duane jerked like a fish on the line, twisting and turning, kicking out. "Let me go!" he shouted. "You have no authority over me." The gun fell from his hand and Leah kicked it away. It slid across the metal floor of the platform and sailed into the gulch.

"Stand still, you idiot." Travis struggled to hold him with one hand. "Take my gun," he ordered Leah. "If he does anything out of line, shoot him."

She took the gun and held it with both hands. It was all very well and good for Travis to tell her to shoot Duane, but any shot she fired had an equal chance of hitting Travis himself, especially with Duane fighting against his restraint like a rabid dog.

"No!" Duane shouted, breaking free of Travis's grasp. He backed up against the cable, his face scarlet, eyes dilated.

"You're trapped, Braeswood," Travis said. "You need to come with me quietly."

"You'll never take me." He glanced over his shoulder, at the narrow trestle over Deadwood Gulch, a picturesque, deep canyon with a silvery creek threading through its rocky floor.

Travis took a step toward him. "Turn around and put your hands behind you," he instructed.

Duane hesitated, then whirled to present his back to the lawman. But instead of standing quietly awaiting the handcuffs, he threw himself over the railing, like a diver intent on plumbing the depths of a lake.

The rumble of the train wheels and the blast of the whistle drowned out any cries Duane might have made when he fell. He bounced awkwardly against the rails, like a mail sack falling from a boxcar, then rolled along the gravel verge and over the edge, falling through space toward the ravine below.

Leah turned away from the horrible sight, one hand clamped over her mouth to cut off a sob. Travis pulled her close. "It's okay," he murmured, stroking her back, much as she had Duane's. "It's over now. We're safe."

Chapter Sixteen

"Did anyone see what happened?" Leah asked when she had recovered enough to speak.

"If they did, we'll know soon," Travis said. "They'll stop the train."

"How could they not have seen?" She pushed away from him and stood on her own, her legs unsteady, but holding her up. "Everyone was looking out the windows."

"But they were watching the scenery, not the goings-on outside a private car," he said.

Instead of stopping, the train began to pick up speed. Already, the trestle over Deadwood

Gulch was receding from view. "Should we tell someone what happened?" Leah asked. "Maybe they can…" Her words trailed away. Maybe they could what? No one could fall that far and survive. If the rocks at the bottom didn't kill him, he had likely drowned in the creek.

"I'll report it when we get to Silverton," he said. "If we say anything now, it will just cause trouble for the train company and a lot of innocent people. Come on, let's go back inside." He took her hand and pulled her toward the door.

"Where's Mr. B?" Marcie asked when they returned to their seats at the table.

"He wanted to say goodbye to someone he knew in one of the other cars," Travis said, delivering the lie as smoothly as if he had practiced. He pulled out a chair for Leah, then sat himself.

"Oh." The young woman looked disappointed. Maybe she had been hoping for a big tip from her high-rolling customer. Leah could have told her not to waste her breath. Duane never tipped well. In his vision of the ideal world, the "little people" served the power brokers of the world, privileged to be part of the machine working for the greater good—or his vision of the greater good.

Travis pulled out the cell phone. "I have a signal," he said.

"Thank God," Leah said. "How soon do you think someone can get to Silverton to pick us up?"

"Someone from the San Juan County Sheriff's Office will be waiting for you at the Silverton Station." Russell Waddell spoke from the open doorway at the end of the car. He moved toward them, the door sliding shut behind him. "I radioed ahead for you."

"What did you tell the sheriff's office?" Travis asked.

"Where's your friend Beaverton?" Waddell asked.

"He stepped back to say goodbye to another friend," Travis said. "He's decided not to take the train for the return trip."

A deep vee formed between the security officer's brows. "Is he really a friend of yours?" he asked. "Neither one of you looked very happy to see him."

"His name isn't even Beaverton," Travis said.

Waddell propped one booted foot on the chair Duane had recently occupied. "Level with me, Agent Steadman. Is Beaverton, or whatever his name is, the fugitive you're after? Do I need to be concerned about the safety of passengers and employees on this train?"

"He isn't a threat to anyone on this train," Travis said.

Not anymore, Leah thought. She closed her eyes and again saw the sickening vision of

Duane falling into that chasm, toward the shallow creek below. As much as she despised the man, the memory of his death made her shudder.

"What did you tell the sheriff's office?" Travis asked Waddell again.

"I told them we'd picked up an FBI agent near Needleton and he needed assistance." Waddell compressed his lips together, as if he had more to say, but was keeping the information to himself for now.

"I appreciate your discretion," Travis said. He held up the phone. "Now if you'll excuse me, I need to contact my bosses and fill them in on the situation."

Waddell gave him a look Leah couldn't interpret. He straightened and nodded to her. "Ma'am."

When they were alone again, except for Marcie, who was cleaning up behind the bar in the corner, Travis phoned his bosses and gave them a brief summary of everything that had happened, including Duane's decision to jump to his death rather than face trial. He listened to the person on the other end for a few seconds, then said goodbye and ended the call.

"They'll contact the San Juan County Sheriff's office and arrange for us to be driven back to Durango," he said. "The rest of the team will meet us there. They'll send a squad into the wilderness area as soon as possible to search for the rest of Braeswood's men."

"What about Duane?" she asked.

"We'll get a recovery team to the gulch tomorrow to claim the body." He covered her hand with his own and squeezed. "The lawman in me wishes I could have brought him in safely and seen him stand trial," he said. "But the rest of me is glad he's dead. He's harmed too many other people in his life, and I could never forgive him for what he did to you."

"I'll just be glad when this is all over," she said. "When I can get back to living a normal life." If she even remembered how.

The train let out three long, low blasts of its whistle. "We're coming into Silverton," Marcie said.

Travis stood and offered his hand to Leah. She let him pull her up and followed him out to the platform. She spotted the trio of sheriff's officers right away, in their khaki pants and shirts and Stetsons, with silver star badges on their chests. Two black-and-white SUVs were parked just behind them. Travis took Leah's hand and started toward them.

"Agent Travis Steadman?" The tallest of the officers, a trim, lean man of forty or so, stepped forward to meet them.

"Yes, sir." Travis offered his credentials.

The lawman glanced at the folder, then returned it and extended his hand. "Sheriff Bryce

Staley, San Juan County," he said. The two other officers moved in beside Leah. "Undersheriff Kinsale and Deputy Lawson."

"Has my office contacted you?" Travis asked.

"Yes, sir," Staley said. "They've filled us in on the situation and provided instructions on how we should handle everything."

"Just get us to Durango," Travis said. "That's all we really need right now."

Staley turned to Leah. "Are you Leah Carlisle?" he asked.

"Yes, sir." She offered a wan smile. "Thank you for helping us out like this."

He didn't return the smile. His gaze flickered to the officers on either side of her and they each grabbed one of her arms. "Leah Carlisle, you are under arrest for conspiracy against the United States." They forced her arms behind her back and the cuffs closed around her wrists, the metal cold against her skin.

Chapter Seventeen

"What do you think you're doing?" Travis charged toward Leah, but Staley pushed between them. "Calm down, Agent Steadman, or I'll have them cuff you, too. We're under direct order from your boss to arrest Ms. Carlisle. We're also under orders to see that you do not interfere."

"You can't arrest her." The words exploded from him with a force he would have preferred to direct to his fists. Leah's eyes locked to his, clouded with fear and confusion, and he wanted to rip apart the men who held her with his bare hands.

"According to your bosses, she's on the FBI's Ten Most Wanted list."

"She's innocent. She's an important witness in my case."

"You can take that up with your supervisors." Staley nodded to his men and they led Leah toward the black-and-white.

"Where are you taking her?" Travis asked.

"She'll be held in the La Plata County Detention Facility in Durango until she can be transferred to Denver, or until someone from the FBI directs us otherwise," Staley said. He put a hand on Travis's shoulder. "Come on. We've got a long drive ahead of us to meet your team in Durango."

He looked back toward Leah. She stopped beside the sheriff's vehicle and her eyes met his. Where he had expected to see the same fear and hopelessness that had clouded her vision when Braeswood made his threats, he found instead a grim determination. For the moment she was battered, but she wasn't defeated, and neither was he. "I'll make some calls and get you out as soon as possible," he called to her.

She nodded, and then one of the deputies pushed down on the top of her head and she folded herself into the backseat of the cruiser.

THE MEMBERS OF Search Team Seven had appropriated one floor of a nondescript office building on the south side of Durango as their base of operations. By the time Travis stormed into the conference room where the team had convened, he had had plenty of time to nurse his anger and worry over the way Leah had been treated. "What the hell are you doing, arresting Leah Carlisle?" he demanded of his commander,

Special Agent in Charge Ted Blessing. "She's a victim here, not a criminal."

"Welcome back, Agent Steadman," Blessing said, his dark Buddha's face as impassive as ever. "I see your temper survived your ordeal in the wilderness."

"You smell worse than my son's entire basketball team after a game," said Special Agent Wade Harris, a fortysomething originally from Montana who had a sixteen-year-old who was apparently a talented defenseman.

"You look as bad as you smell," Special Agent Cameron Hsung said.

Travis ignored the gibes and continued to stare at Blessing. A twenty-year veteran of the Bureau, Blessing never let anything ruffle him. And Travis had never known the man to act rashly. But arresting Leah defied all logic. "I told you on the phone she was innocent," he said. "Braeswood kidnapped and murdered her sister, stole her property, and practically made her his slave."

"All assertions that we will thoroughly investigate," Blessing said. "But the fact remains that until we have proof of any of this, she's a wanted fugitive, a suspected terrorist and a flight risk. We followed the same procedure for her that we would follow with any other person in her position. She'll have ample opportunity to prove her innocence at a later date."

"I vouched for her. Doesn't that count for anything?" he said.

Blessing leveled his gaze at him. "You had a long-term, close relationship with Ms. Carlisle, the nature of which, I note, you did not fully divulge," he said.

Travis didn't flinch. "I told you I knew her, and that we went to school together. I didn't lie."

"Are you familiar with the term 'sins of omission'?" Blessing shook his head. "That's all beside the point now. But I don't think it's unreasonable to conclude that your judgment might be clouded by the fact that you were once engaged to marry the woman."

Travis shot a look at Luke, who shrugged and looked guilty. The two of them would talk later. He turned his attention back to Blessing. "There's nothing wrong with my judgment," he said. "Leah is innocent."

"And she is perfectly safe where she is right now." Blessing put a hand on his shoulder, his gaze locked on Travis's. There was sympathy in those dark brown eyes, as well as the stern concern of a father for a troubled son. "You've had a rough four days. I'm ordering you to go home and get a shower, a good meal and a decent night's sleep. I want you fresh and ready in the morning to take the train with the rest of us to Needleton Station. We still have a number of Braeswood's associates to pick up."

"You're waiting until the morning?" Travis asked. "Why not go right away?"

"The tourist train is the only way into the area where we believe the men are located. Unless you want to make a multiday hike over rough, roadless terrain."

"Then send the train in tonight," Travis said. "Don't give them all night to get away."

Blessing grimaced. "You can't exactly sneak into an area on a steam train. They'll hear us coming from miles away. We've commandeered a car on the first morning train. We're posing as a group of friends on a hiking trip."

"What about Braeswood's body?" Travis asked.

"We've got a recovery team on the second train that will handle retrieving it," Blessing said. "They'll transport it to the La Plata County Coroner."

"You said he jumped from the train?" Agent Harris asked. "How did that happen?"

The others gathered around him. "Leah distracted him by pointing out a gold mine in the mountains above the tracks," Travis said. "He'd gotten cocky, believing we were subdued and trapped. He let down his guard and I grabbed him. I was trying to cuff him when he fought me off. I had him cornered and was trying to persuade him to come with me quietly when he jumped."

"Any chance he survived?" Agent Hsung asked.

Travis shook his head. "No way. He fell at least four hundred feet into a rocky, shallow creek."

"Without him, we might have a harder time making a case against the others," Luke said.

"Leah can help us there," Travis said. "She lived in the same household for six months. She doesn't know everything Braeswood was up to, but she can identify many of the people who worked with him. And we've got the house outside of Durango. That might turn up documents or computer files that could link Braeswood to his crimes."

"No luck with the house," Harris said. "They torched it."

"Probably cleaned it out before they set the blaze," Hsung said.

"They burned Gus's body along with the house," Wade said, his expression grim.

For the first time since rejoining the team, Travis realized Agent Gus Mathers wasn't with them. Neither was Jack Prescott. He remembered the khaki-clad figure he'd seen lying in front of the house. "They killed Gus?" he asked.

"He was trying to get to the van and they gunned him down," Blessing said.

"What about Jack?" Travis asked.

"He was injured when we fled from the house into the woods," Hsung said.

"He took a couple of bullets," Blessing said. "He'll recover, but for now he's on medical leave."

Travis swore under his breath. Another murder Braeswood was responsible for. "You need to let Leah out of jail," he said. "She can help us stop these guys before they act again."

"She'll have her chance to prove her innocence," Blessing said. "I want to stop these terrorists as badly as you do, but we're going to do this the right way. No slick lawyer or tabloid journalist is going to accuse us of favoritism or taking shortcuts. When we send these guys away, they're going for life."

He turned to agent Luke Renfro, Travis's closest friend on the team. "Agent Renfro, take Agent Steadman home. He needs to get some rest. And frankly, I can't stand the smell of him any longer."

SAN JUAN COUNTY, COLORADO, didn't have the population to support a jail of its own, so the San Juan County Sheriff's officers escorted Leah to the La Plata County Detention Facility in Durango, where she was photographed and fingerprinted. She was allowed to take a shower and dressed in loose orange scrubs. She could have wept with joy as the hot water and soap washed away days of sweat and grime, but instead she shed tears of anger and frustration. She had known she was wanted as an accomplice of Duane's, but she had never actually believed the authorities would arrest her. She was with Travis, and he would explain that she was innocent, a victim, not a criminal.

But Travis had been helpless when the sheriff's deputies handcuffed her and led her away. Speaking up for her might even jeopardize his career. She was on her own again, stranded in a strange world full of enemies. She would have to learn how to cope, as she had when she was with Duane. At least here she didn't have to worry about the daily threat of rape and violence—she hoped.

Alone in her cell, segregated from the general population of the jail, she lay on the hard bunk and tried to sleep. Maybe when she woke up, she would discover this was all a horrible nightmare, a variation on the familiar theme of being trapped and helpless. But, exhausted as she was, sleep eluded her. When she had lost Travis the first time, she had grieved hard, but had eventually resigned herself to the loss. He was better off—safer—without her in his life.

Being with him again had made her believe they had a second chance at happiness. To have that chance snatched away hurt even more than the first loss, a sorrow too deep for tears.

"You don't look like I thought a terrorist would."

She sat up and stared at the man who spoke—a young guard with buzzed hair and a prominent Adam's apple. His name tag identified him simply as Lawson.

"I'm not a terrorist," she said.

He ignored her plea of innocence. Probably everyone who came here claimed not to have committed their crime, she reasoned. "What makes you hate this country so much you want to destroy it?" he asked.

"I don't hate this country," she said.

"That's not what I heard."

"When do I leave here?" she asked. She had already had enough of this guy.

"Don't know. I guess the Feds are still arguing over where to send you. Maybe you'll go to Denver, maybe you'll go to Washington—or maybe somewhere else. Wherever you end up, the penalty for treason is the same." He made a slashing motion across his throat.

She knew she shouldn't rise to his bait, but she couldn't keep quiet any longer. "The FBI agent I was with when I was arrested will vouch for me," she said. "He knows I'm innocent."

"Some men will say anything for a pretty face and figure." Lawson looked her up and down. "There's no accounting for taste."

She lay down again and turned her back to him. Duane had said worse to her—much worse. His abuse wasn't anything she would have ever thanked him for, but at least he had helped her develop a thick skin. Something that would come in handy in the days ahead.

LUKE INSISTED ON coming inside the apartment Travis had rented in a complex that housed several of the team members on temporary assignment in Durango. After only four days standing empty, the air in the place smelled stale. "Thanks for bringing me home," Travis said when they both stood in the one-bedroom unit's entryway. "I won't keep you."

"I'll stick around a while." Luke slipped off the light jacket he wore against the evening mountain chill and dropped it over the back of the cheap beige sofa that had come with the furnished unit. "Want me to order a pizza while you shower?"

No. He didn't want a pizza and he didn't want to talk to anyone about what had happened—not even his best friend. But his stomach growled at the mention of pizza, and the prospect of a long evening spent pacing the floor while he worried about Leah was too bleak to contemplate. "Yes, sure," he said. "But what about Morgan?" Luke had met the pretty sports reporter while the team worked a terrorism case in Denver a couple of months ago and the two had been an item ever since. She had followed him to Durango, and they were planning a spring wedding.

"She understands about my work."

Travis narrowed his eyes at his friend. "So I'm work now? Did Blessing ask you to pick my brain?"

"Morgan understands about friends, too," Luke said. "And Blessing didn't tell me anything but to bring you home."

"And to make sure I stayed here. Don't worry. I'm too beat to go anywhere." The only person he wanted to see was in jail and the sheriff wouldn't let him anywhere near her. He might as well stay home and rest up for tomorrow.

"Hit the shower," Travis said. "I'll call for the pizza."

Half an hour later, showered, shampooed and shaved, wearing clean clothes and feeling better than he had in days, Travis dived into the large sausage and pepperoni pizza Luke had ordered.

"I had dreams about a pizza like this while I was out there," he said, wiping sauce off his chin. "And steak and cheeseburgers and cherry pie."

"I've always been partial to peach pie, myself." Luke polished off the last bite of crust from his first slice of pizza.

"I've never been so hungry in my life," Travis said.

"Were you ever worried you wouldn't make it?" Luke asked.

"The first night was bad, when we knew Braeswood's men were chasing us. But once we spotted the train and knew which way to go, it was just a matter of slogging it out."

"How did Leah do?" Luke asked.

"Leah was amazing. I know grown men—trained agents—who would have cracked under the pressure she was under, but she didn't. She never complained, either. She just kept going."

"Not what I expected," Luke said. He moved a piece of pizza onto his plate and contemplated it.

"You told Blessing she and I had been engaged, didn't you?" Travis asked.

"It was going to come out," Luke said. "Maybe not right away, but a reporter would have dug it up eventually. And I thought the information was relevant. Blessing did, too."

"Yeah. I probably would have done the same in your position."

Luke gave him a questioning look. "None of my business, but are you two an item again? Even after she dumped you?"

Were they? He wanted to try again with Leah, but was that even possible? "She dumped me because she was afraid Braeswood would kill me," Travis blurted. He hadn't meant to discuss this with anyone, but now the need to tell someone overwhelmed that reticence. "She stayed with Braeswood because he had kidnapped her sister. He took over all her assets and made her a prisoner. Then he killed her sister and made her believe if she left him, he would hunt her down and kill her."

Luke let out a low whistle. "She told you all this?"

"I believe her, Luke. And her sister is dead. I remember reading the obituary a few weeks after Leah left." His first instinct had been to call Leah and offer his condolences, but then he had realized he had no idea how to reach her. Her apartment had been rented by a stranger, and her cell phone number no longer worked. She had made it clear that she wanted nothing to do with him and had done everything to make sure he couldn't find her. "I should have known something was up when she broke our engagement," he said. "That wasn't her. She was always so open and straightforward. If she had really wanted to leave me, she would have told me to my face, not in some 'Dear John' letter left on the kitchen table."

"So why didn't she tell you to your face?" Luke asked. "Why didn't she ask you to help her, instead of running away like that?"

"Because she was afraid for her younger sister. She thought if she did everything Braeswood asked, he would leave Sarah alone. He did let her go after Leah turned over everything she owned to him. But he arranged for Sarah to have an 'accident' not long after."

"How do you know it wasn't really an accident? One with really bad timing?"

"Apparently Braeswood got a charge out of telling Leah what he had done to her sister. It was another way he played with her mind and made her believe he had total control over her life."

"Why did he pick on Leah?" Luke pointed a slice of pizza at him. "What's the connection?"

Travis shook his head. "I don't know. She worked for Senator Wilson, who was head of the Senate Committee on Homeland Security. Braeswood used Leah to try to get to the senator. But if that was all he wanted, he didn't have to keep using her the way he did. Maybe he wanted something in her assets. Her parents left her a lot of money and property when they died. Or maybe he saw her one day and was attracted and decided she would be the target of his sick game."

"We need to find out why he targeted Leah," Luke said. "It could be important."

"I'm not going to let it drop, if that's what you think," Travis said. "But first, I have to get the charges against her dismissed. She's no more a terrorist than you or I. And she can be a big help to us in this case. She knows Braeswood and the people he worked with better than anyone at this point."

"If she knew about his planned attacks and she never turned him in to the authorities, that could be a big strike against her," Luke said. "Enough to get her some serious jail time."

"She didn't know any of that," Travis said. "He made sure she was kept in the dark."

"Still, it's going to be tough," Luke said. "No judge or other elected official wants to look like he's soft on terrorists."

"She's not a terrorist!" He slammed his fist on the table, making their water glasses jump.

"Okay. Calm down." Luke sat back, looking thoughtful. "I've got a lawyer friend we can call. He might be able to persuade the courts to release Leah on bond."

"Call your friend," Travis said. "But you said it yourself. No judge wants to be seen as going soft on terrorists."

"It would help if we could get Blessing on

our side," Luke said. "A special agent in charge vouching for her would carry a lot of weight."

"Fat chance of that," Travis said. He sat back also, suddenly bone weary. "Blessing is the one who gave the order for her to be arrested in the first place. He's never going to back off of that."

"He might surprise you," Luke said. "He plays by the book, but he's not above writing new chapters when it suits his purpose."

AFTER LUKE LEFT, Travis wouldn't have believed he would sleep a wink. He lay in bed, imagining Leah in a stark cell, with no blanket or mattress and a lightbulb that burned twenty-four hours a day. Here in his own comfortable bed it seemed a betrayal for him to get a good night's sleep.

But sleep he did. He woke at six when his alarm blared, took another shower, had two bowls of stale cereal for breakfast and went to meet the rest of the team at the train station.

He recognized a few of the workers—the conductor, Russell Waddell and Marcie—from the previous day's trip, but they made no show of recognizing him. They had probably been thoroughly prepped on the importance of secrecy.

The five active members of Search Team Seven and four other agents brought in to help with this mission rode together in an open gondola car near the rear of the train. In keeping with their cover story of a group of friends on a hiking trip, they had stashed loaded backpacks in the cargo hold and wore stout boots, hats, cargo pants and long-sleeved T-shirts under light fleece jackets.

"This is incredible scenery." Cameron Hsung swiveled his head from side to side, trying to take in everything as the train chugged out of Durango, headed for the mountains.

"It gets better the farther we go," Travis said. But he could muster little enthusiasm for the journey. The thought of hiking through the woods again made every part of him ache, and every step would be just one more reminder that this time Leah wasn't with them.

"How are we going to find the guys we're looking for?" Wade Harris asked as the train chugged along beside the highway, blasting its whistle at every crossing.

"Agent Steadman, perhaps you'd like to address that question." Special Agent in Charge Blessing, dressed like the others in hiking gear, wearing mirrored wraparound sunglasses that made him look more like a Secret Service agent and less like a vacationer, turned to Travis.

"You'll recognize them," Travis said. "And not just because you've probably seen some of them before. They're wearing black tactical gear and they move like trained fighters. Not to mention your average hiker isn't armed to the teeth. These guys have sidearms and semiautomatic rifles, and I suspect at least some of them are wearing body armor."

"How many of them are there?" Luke asked.

"We think at least eight," Travis said. "The last time I saw any of them was the day before yesterday. They were chasing us and we managed to evade them. We overheard two of them stating the plan was to watch the bridge for our approach, since that was the best way to get to the train, and the train was our fastest ticket out of the wilderness. They knew we had no food or supplies and that we were getting desperate."

"You could have walked out the way you came in," Blessing said.

"That would have taken days," Travis said. "But I imagine Braeswood was smart enough to have men watching that route, too."

"I can't believe he went and offed himself," Wade said. "After all these months of us chasing him, he went and cheated us out of putting him on trial. Where's the justice in that?"

"Ending up on the rocks at the bottom of a ravine isn't exactly an easy way to go," Luke said.

"Tell the truth, Travis." Cameron Hsung leaned forward to address Travis. "When you had him backed up to the drop-off, weren't you tempted—at least a little—to give him a little push?"

Travis had thought Leah might push Braeswood. He had a clear image of her hand on his back, the determination mixed with pain in her face. Maybe he should have let her do it. After the torture Braeswood had put her through, it would have been fitting.

But he wasn't wired that way. He had been taught to protect all life, even that of the criminals. So he had moved in quickly to put on the cuffs. Just not quickly enough. "I wanted to make him go through a trial and endure the public scorn he deserved," he said. "That would have been a fitting punishment. Then I wanted to see him rot in prison for the rest of his life."

"It would have been good to find out what his plans were," Blessing said. "It's possible he's already set in motion other acts of terrorism and his followers will carry them out." He directed one of his patented stern looks at Travis. "Do you think Ms. Carlisle can tell us anything about Braeswood's planned activities?"

If Travis said yes, it might be Leah's ticket to freedom from jail, at least for a little while. But he wouldn't lie to his boss. "She says Braeswood tried to keep her in the dark about his activities. He had thugs who guarded her, and he conducted his business meetings away from the house or in his home office, where she wasn't allowed to go. The best she can do is give us an idea of his whereabouts for the past six months, and identify people he associated with. That might lead us to other sources of information."

"Agent Renfro and I did some research last night and the story she gave you checks out," Blessing said. "At least as far as the surface facts. She did resign from her job and sign over all her property to Braeswood, or more accurately, to one of the shell corporations we suspect he had set up to launder money for his terrorist activities. Her sister died in a car accident three weeks later. It was a one-car accident that local police labeled as vehicular suicide, but I found notes by one investigator that noted the evidence was inconclusive and, in his opinion, suspicious."

"Did anyone ever follow up on that?" Travis asked.

Blessing shook his head. "You know how it is. An overworked department has better things to do than follow up on every bit of information that doesn't line up quite right, especially if no family members or press are on their backs about it."

Travis looked at Luke, who held out his hands in a gesture of contrition. "I had to check it out," he said. "For your peace of mind, as well as ours."

Good thing he had, too. Travis owed his friend one. "Does this mean you'll go to bat for Leah?" he asked Blessing.

"We'll do what we can," Blessing said. "The Justice Department is a separate entity. They're under no obligation to listen to us."

But they will, Travis thought. *They have to.*

Chapter Eighteen

The sun had already disappeared behind the canyon walls when the team members returned to the Needleton Station late that afternoon after the last tourist train had departed, a row of shackled prisoners in tow. They had taken Braeswood's men by surprise. Only one had escaped through the woods, and local authorities and train personnel had been alerted to be on the lookout for him.

The chase had been cathartic for Travis. Once on the hunt, his aches and pains had vanished. He had been able to home in on the area where they had seen the men and positively identify each of them. The outlaws fought back against the agents, but only briefly, outmatched and outnumbered. The days in the woods had taken their toll on Braeswood's men—they looked like refugees of some tragedy, unshaven and dirty, their clothes rumpled and torn. Travis realized he must have looked like this when he'd emerged from the woods. No wonder the train passengers had stared.

No passengers stared as they boarded cars for the return trip. Federal authorities had commissioned a special train consisting of only two passenger cars and an engine to take the prisoners back to Durango. Instead of a conductor, Russell Waddell met them at the top of the platform in the first car. "You're looking a little different today, Agent Steadman," he said with a grin.

"I imagine this is more excitement than you

usually see on your tourist train," Travis said as the prisoners filed past.

"You might be surprised," Waddell said. "Our main focus is on tourist traffic, but we've hauled everyone from Hollywood stars to construction equipment and a whole herd of bighorn sheep."

"No sheep today." Travis nodded to the row of disheveled men slouched in the train seats. "Though I think most of the fight has gone out of them."

"What happened yesterday, after you got to Silverton?" Waddell asked. "Did you arrest Beaverton, or whatever his name is?"

Travis tried to keep the pain he felt from his face. He didn't like remembering the scene in Silverton, or the look on Leah's face as the sheriff's deputies hauled her away. "It's a long story," he said. "But Mr. Beaverton won't be causing any more trouble."

As the train whistle sounded and the cars

lurched forward, he dumped his pack in an empty seat with several others, then made his way to the front of the car to sit beside Luke. "I thought we were headed back to Durango," Luke said. "But we're traveling the wrong direction."

"I think we're stopping off at Deadwood Gulch to pick up the recovery team," Travis said.

"The place where Braeswood jumped?"

"Yeah." A man had to be crazy to do something like that.

They fell silent, Travis staring at his own reflection in the window against the blackness outside. All day he had been distracted by the mission, but now his thoughts turned to Leah. What was she doing right now? Did she think he had abandoned her again?

The train slowed, then jerked to a stop with a loud exhalation of steam from the brakes. After a few moments, they heard voices, and a quartet of weary men filed into the car. They conferred among themselves, then they moved down the aisle, toward Travis. "Are you Agent Steadman?" one asked.

"I'm Travis Steadman."

"Shawn Peterborough." The man offered his hand. "San Juan County Search and Rescue. We contracted to bring up a body from Deadwood Gulch."

"Was he in bad shape?" Luke asked.

Peterborough shook his head. "He wasn't in any kind of shape. We couldn't find him."

Travis stared, trying to let this information sink in. "What do you mean, you couldn't find him? I saw him fall from the train into that gulch. Nobody could survive a drop like that."

"We didn't find anything—no blood, no footprints, nothing," Peterborough said. "We spent all day combing through the area for two miles on every side. Nothing. Your guy is gone."

That was impossible. "Maybe an animal dragged the body away," Travis said. "A wolf or a mountain lion."

"We don't have wolves here," Peterborough said. "And mountain lions store their prey near the kill site. We would have found it."

"He couldn't have survived a fall like that," Travis said.

"I've seen stranger things happen," Peterborough said. "If he landed in a deeper part of the creek, in softer mud, and if he was very, very lucky…" He shrugged. "He might have walked away with a few bruises, maybe a broken bone or two."

"Son of a—" Travis bit off the curse. "He can't have gotten away. He can't have."

"If you want, we can go in tomorrow with a search dog," Peterborough said. "But the trail will be pretty cold by then. We'd have to get lucky to find anything."

"Nothing about this mission has been lucky," Luke said.

"Yeah, well, even if your guy survived his fall and walked into the woods, he's not going to last long out there alone with no supplies," Peterborough said.

"I'm sure he had a phone," Travis said. "He wouldn't have had to walk far toward Silverton to be able to call for help. He could even follow the train tracks to town. It's only a few miles from the gulch."

"Provided the phone wasn't damaged in the fall, and he was in any shape to climb up to the tracks," Peterborough said. "I made some calls, and no one in town reported a man wandering in from the wilderness."

"Maybe they didn't notice him, with all the tourists and everything," Travis said. "And Braeswood already had a car and driver waiting in Silverton. He could have met up with them and been out of town before the train left to return to Durango."

"If he did make it out of here alive, we'll find out sooner or later," Luke said. "He won't stay quiet for long."

"That's what I'm afraid of," Travis said. "When we do hear from Braeswood again, it won't be good."

AFTER TWO NIGHTS in jail, Leah had decided that being patient and cooperative wasn't getting her anywhere. She was fed up with the guards' condescending attitudes and their assumption that she was guilty of the charges against her. She didn't want to hear any more excuses about why she was being held here in the middle of nowhere, with no access to a lawyer or any outside visitors. She refused to believe Travis hadn't at least tried to see her, so her jailers must be keeping him away, the way they were keeping away the reporters and others who had tried to speak with her.

"You have to let me see a lawyer," she said when a guard responded to her shouts for help on the morning after her second night in the stark, uncomfortable cell.

"You'll see a lawyer whenever you get to Denver or DC or wherever they decide to send you," the guard—a portly redhead whose name badge identified him as Erickson—said.

"You can't just hold me here forever," she said.

"We can do whatever the Feds tell us to do," Erickson said, and turned away.

"Then bring me some paper and a pen," she called after him.

"Why?" He turned toward her again. "Do you plan to write your memoirs?"

"I'm going to write a letter," she said. The *Denver Post* wouldn't pass up the chance to publish a letter from a notorious fugitive who'd been captured, she was sure.

Maybe she would write to Travis, too. She would apologize for dragging him into this mess, and tell him she loved him. She hadn't had the courage to say the words out loud when he was awake when they were in the wilderness, but she wanted him to know them now. Whatever happened, whether they were able to ever be together again, she wanted him to know she loved him, and she always had.

The writing paper never materialized, however. Instead, about ten o'clock Erickson returned with another officer, who unlocked her cell and motioned for her to step out. "Someone here to see you," he said.

"Who is it?" she asked as he led her through the double doors that separated the cells from the rest of the facility.

But he ignored the question and motioned her

366 Lawman on the Hunt

to walk in front of him down the hall, into a gray, windowless room that contained a table and a single chair.

He left her in the room, locking the door behind him. She sat in the chair and looked up at the camera mounted in the ceiling. Was someone watching her now, the way a scientist watches a rat in a maze, waiting to see how the animal will react to various stimuli?

After what felt like an hour had passed, but was probably only ten minutes or so, the lock on the door snapped and the doorknob turned. She stood to greet her visitors. A distinguished-looking black man in a dark suit entered first, but it was the second man who commanded all Leah's attention. "Travis!" she said, and started toward him.

She would have hugged him, but he held her at arm's length. "How are you doing?" he asked, looking her up and down.

"I'm okay." She glanced down at the baggy orange scrubs and rubber flip-flops they had given her to wear. "At least I'm cleaner than the last time you saw me."

"Ms. Carlisle, I am Special Agent in Charge Ted Blessing," the black man said, "with the Federal Bureau of Investigation. Special Agent Steadman and I have some questions for you about your association with Duane Braeswood."

She looked from Travis to Agent Blessing and took a step back. So they were here in an official capacity, not because Travis hadn't been able to stay away. No wonder he was being so distant and formal. She returned to the chair and sat, smoothing her palms down her thighs. "I'm happy to answer any questions you have," she said. "But shouldn't I have a lawyer present?"

"You're entitled to a lawyer," Blessing said. "We will see that one is provided when we question you in our offices later this afternoon."

She turned to Travis, afraid to jump to any conclusions. "Are you taking me to Washington?" she asked.

"We have offices here in Durango," he said. "But for now, you're being released into my custody, pending disposition of the charges against you."

She wet her lips, choosing her words carefully, and decided to address her next question to Agent Blessing. "What is the disposition of the charges against me?"

"We've petitioned the US attorney's office to drop the charges against you in exchange for your cooperation with us in this case."

The breath rushed out of her and she was glad she was sitting down. "I'm happy to cooperate," she said again, though inside she wanted to whoop for joy.

"Come on." Travis offered his hand. "Let's get you out of here."

Ten minutes later, she stood on the street in front of the jail with Travis and Agent Blessing. She still wore the orange jail scrubs, and was aware of the stares of passersby. But her own clothes, which they had offered to return to her, were too filthy to contemplate putting on again. "We'll get you some new clothes," Travis said as he opened the back door of the car for her.

She had hoped he would ride in the backseat with her, but he slid into the front passenger seat, and Blessing drove. The short drive across town was largely silent, with the men exchanging a few bland comments about the scenery or the weather. Neither of them said anything to her, as if she weren't even there.

She stared at the back of Travis's head, wishing she knew what he was thinking. Was he trying to distance himself from his involvement with her because he worried what their relationship might mean to his career? In the hours they had been apart, had doubts about her innocence grown? Or was he merely concerned with looking professional in front of his boss?

Yet he had said she was being released into his custody. That meant he was responsible for her, didn't it? Why would he accept such responsibility if he didn't believe in her?

At some point during the long drive, she dozed, lulled by the warm sun on her face and the car's comfortable backseat. She woke when the car stopped in front of a small apartment complex, the front of the building landscaped with beds of flowers and groupings of evergreens. "We have a meeting with someone from the US attorney's office at three," Agent Blessing said as Travis opened the car door.

"Yes, sir," Travis said. "We'll be there." He climbed out of the car, then opened Leah's door for her. "Come with me."

She exited the car and followed him up the

walkway toward the building. Blessing drove away and Travis took out a key and led the way to a door on the second floor. "I rented the place furnished," he said. "So it's not much."

"Where are we?" she asked, confused.

"This is my apartment," he said.

"Why did you bring me here?"

"'Released into my custody' means I'm responsible for you. You have to stay with me." He frowned at her. "I thought you understood that."

"So I'm your prisoner."

"No." He shoved open the door and motioned for her to go inside ahead of him.

He was right when he had said the apartment was plain. The front room was small and decorated in neutral colors and nondescript furniture—the kind used in midgrade hotel rooms. But it looked comfortable and it wasn't a jail cell. She stood a few feet inside the room, unsure what to do next.

Travis closed the door and stood still also, looking as unsure as she felt. "You're not my prisoner," he said. "I don't want you to think of it that way."

"I'm not free to leave," she said.

"Do you want to leave?" He looked pained.

She turned away. "I don't know what I want," she said softly. But she did know. She wanted him to look at her with eyes of love again. She wanted to feel his arms around her and hear him tell her that everything would be all right.

He moved toward her, but stopped when he was still a few feet away. "I know this isn't the best situation," he said. "It's not what I want, but it's the best we can do right now. It was a compromise to get you out of jail."

She nodded, tears clogging her throat. She swallowed and found her voice. "Thank you for getting me out of there," she said.

"We're going to get the charges dropped," he

said. "We captured most of the men who were with Braeswood in the wilderness and at least two of them are cooperating. They confirmed that you weren't involved in Braeswood's terrorist activities, and that they were sent to hunt you and me in the woods." He laid his hand on her shoulder, the weight of it so heavy—physically and emotionally—she feared her knees might buckle. "Agent Blessing checked out your story, as much as he could, and he believes you're innocent now, too. The US attorney will listen to him."

"Is Agent Blessing your boss?" she asked.

"Yes. He's a hard man, but a fair one."

"Did he order you to look after me? Is this your punishment for associating with a wanted fugitive?"

"A punishment? What are you talking about?"

"It's clear you don't want to be seen with me,"

she said. "You've scarcely looked at me since we left the jail."

He moved closer still, one hand remaining on her shoulder, the other under her chin, nudging her head up to look at him. "I couldn't look at you without wanting to touch you. I had to be careful in front of Blessing and others who might be watching. There were reporters outside the jail, you know."

She shook her head. "I didn't know."

"They were across the street, taking pictures. Until the charges against you are dropped, we have to be careful. If the press thinks you received preferential treatment because of your personal relationship with an FBI agent, it could jeopardize not only your freedom, but the whole case. Do you understand?"

"Yes." Everything he said made sense, difficult as it was to hear.

"But we don't have to be careful now," he said.

"We're alone." He bent and covered her lips with his own.

The kiss began gently, but she wrapped her arms around him, pulling him close and letting him feel her desperate need of him. "I was so afraid," she whispered when at last they broke the kiss.

"It tore me apart, seeing them take you away in cuffs," he said. "I hated thinking of you in that cell, alone and afraid."

"I wasn't afraid of jail," she said. "At least, not much." She stroked her fingers along his jaw. "I was afraid I'd lost you."

"You haven't lost me," he said. "Never again." He kissed her cheek, then drew away. "I bought you some clothes and things. They're in the bathroom. You can take a shower and get dressed and when you come out, I'll have lunch ready."

"That sounds good," she said, suddenly aware of her uncombed hair and baggy orange scrubs.

In the bathroom she found jeans, a gauzy blouse, new underwear, a pair of leather flats and silver hoop earrings. She smiled, touched that he had not only remembered her size, but the styles she liked. In the shower, a new bottle of her brand of shampoo and vanilla-scented shower gel awaited. She let the water run until it was steamy, then indulged in the luxury of standing under the spray until she had washed away the scent and feel of the jail. When she finally emerged, her hair blow-dried and her face freshened with the powder, mascara and lipstick he had also purchased, she felt like a new woman.

Travis looked up from the table he was setting and smiled. "You look like you feel better," he said.

She hugged him. "I feel great. Thanks for the clothes and makeup. And the earrings." She touched the silver hoops. "You still remember what I like."

He looked pleased. "Sit down," he said. "I don't know about you, but I'm still making up for all those lost meals."

She sat in the chair he indicated and he set a plate in front of her—a bacon-wrapped fillet, baked potato and green beans. "I'd pour you a glass of wine, but we probably shouldn't show up at the courthouse this afternoon smelling of alcohol," he said.

"This looks fabulous." She inhaled the aroma of the steak, and her mouth watered.

He sat across from her. "Dig in."

For long minutes, neither of them said anything as they ate. Finally, her hunger abated, she set down her fork and looked at him. "What's going to happen this afternoon?" she asked.

"Your attorney will be there." He wiped his mouth with a napkin. "My friend Luke knew a good criminal defense attorney, so we called him. Reg Kosinski. He's meeting us there. He'll present the motion to drop the charges. Agent Blessing will say his piece and hopefully that will be it."

"Agent Blessing said he wanted to question me."

"Yes. You can ask your lawyer to sit in on that if you want, but once the charges are dropped, it shouldn't be necessary. All we want is to hear your story and anything you can tell us that might help us find and convict Braeswood."

She froze in the act of reaching for her water glass. "What do you mean find Braeswood? Isn't he dead?"

Travis shook his head. "The search-and-rescue team we sent into Deadwood Gulch couldn't find any sign of him."

"But he jumped from the train. How could he have survived a fall like that?"

"The search-and-rescue guy I talked to thinks he could have made it." He took a long drink. "Anything you can tell us will help us figure out his next move."

"I'll do my best." She shivered. "I hate to think of him out there somewhere." She wouldn't feel safe until he was locked up for good.

"Don't worry," Travis said. "I won't let him hurt you ever again."

"It's strange, being away from him after so long," she said. "I'm thrilled, but I'm a little nervous about starting over. I have so much to do. Find a job, an apartment and a car. I don't have any money or anything. It's a little daunting."

"You're strong and you're smart. You'll get through this."

"I will." She took a deep breath. "I just have to figure out where to start."

"Blessing thinks there's a chance we can recover at least some of your assets from Braeswood. And I'll help you with anything else you need."

"I can't let you do that," she said. "You shouldn't—"

He reached across the table and took her hand. "I'm going to help the woman I love," he said. He rubbed his thumb across her knuckles, sending heat curling through her. "The woman I want to marry."

Her breath caught and she stared at him. "What are you saying?"

He reached into his pocket and pulled out a ring. The diamond solitaire glinted in the sunlight through the window behind her. He slid the ring onto the third finger of her left hand. "I believe this belongs here," he said.

She stared at the ring, as she had stared at it so many times in the weeks after their engagement. "You kept it," she said.

"I did."

"I was sure you'd be so angry with me for re-turning it that you'd sell it or throw it away."

"I had to keep it," he said. "Just in case I got the chance to win you back."

She didn't remember rising from her chair and moving around the table toward him, but the next thing she knew she was sitting in his lap, his arms around her. "Leah Carlisle, will you marry me?" he asked.

"Yes." She kissed him, joyful tears wetting both their cheeks. "I love you," she said. "I never stopped loving you."

"No," he said. "And we will never stop."

Charges Dropped Against Suspected Terrorist

The federal government has dropped all charges against a woman who had been sus-pected of participation in a terrorist cell re-sponsible for dozens of deaths around the world. Leah Carlisle, 27, was placed on the FBI's Ten Most Wanted List earlier this year after a link was established between her and suspected cell leader Duane Braeswood. Ms. Carlisle was captured in a raid on Braeswood's compound in rural La Plata County last week. "We have evidence that Ms. Carlisle was not, in fact, a member of the terrorist cell," said FBI Special Agent in Charge Theodore Blessing in a statement to the press. "Rather, she was kidnapped and held hostage by Braeswood and kept a prisoner until she managed to escape during the raid on a rental home where Braeswood and his followers were staying. She has fully cooperated with authorities and is providing valuable information we hope will lead to the arrest and conviction of Braeswood and his followers."

FBI Special Agent Gus Mathers was killed

in the raid on the Braeswood compound, and another agent was wounded. Several members of the suspected terrorist group escaped, including Braeswood. A subsequent fire destroyed the home where the group had been staying. Six members of the group were captured in the Weminuche Wilderness. Braeswood and one other of his associates are still at large.

* * * * *